Sir John Bowring

Hwa tsien ki. The Flowery Scroll

A Chinese Novel

Sir John Bowring

Hwa tsien ki. The Flowery Scroll
A Chinese Novel

ISBN/EAN: 9783337030872

Printed in Europe, USA, Canada, Australia, Japan

Cover: Foto ©Andreas Hilbeck / pixelio.de

More available books at **www.hansebooks.com**

HWA TSIEN KI.

THE FLOWERY SCROLL:

𝔄 Chinese 𝔑ovel.

TRANSLATED AND ILLUSTRATED WITH NOTES

BY

SIR JOHN BOWRING, LL.D., F.R.S.

LATE H.B.M. PLENIPOTENTIARY IN CHINA; PRESIDENT OF THE CHINESE BRANCH
OF THE ROYAL ASIATIC SOCIETY; PHRA MAHA YESA OF SIAM, ETC. ETC.

LONDON:

WM. H. ALLEN & CO., 13, WATERLOO PLACE,
PALL MALL, S.W.

1868.

PREFACE.

THE translation of the *Chinese Courtship*, by Mr. P. P. Thoms, published by the E. I. C. Press, at Macao, in 1824, and presenting, with the original text, a lineal rendering of the popular novel, was a great service rendered to the students of the Chinese language; but it appeared to me, that a more free and flowing version, with reference to other editions than that so employed, might have greater attractions for the English reader, and give opportunities for the introduction of explanatory notes and observations, suggested by a long residence in China, and by many opportunities of access to that inner life, in which the national character can alone be seen, and which was wholly unobtainable half a century ago. Mr.

Schlegel, who has printed, in the transactions of the Batavian Society of Arts and Sciences, 1865, an excellent translation, under the title of " *Geschiedenis van het gebloemde Brief Papier*," has also avoided the metrical form of the original, which necessarily gives a certain stiffness to the style.   He has adopted the common narrative form.

No apology is, however, necessary for preserving the general phraseology of the story. "If," as is said, "the individual style is the individual man," the national style is the nation, and it is emphatically so in China, where all thoughts, feelings and expressions, are moulded to a common type,—that type being the result of a universally similar education, in which the elementary books employed are invariably the same.

The character of that national education may be seen in those constant references to the ancient legends of the central kingdom,—in that language, so flowery, poetical and fanciful, an intimacy with which is regarded as evidence of the highest refinement of manners and of the most elevated intellectual cultivation. Even the State Papers of China are permeated with these elements.

On one occasion, a Mandarin said to me that, " the proof of your being no better than barbarians, is, that you have no poetry in your language." No doubt, our dispatches seemed to them repulsively dry. In correspondence with the Tae Ping Kings, one of them asked whether I had ever received any "poetry," written by the hand of God,—and assured me that he had "autograph verses" sent to him direct by a messenger from heaven.

The notes appended to the Chapters may seem profuse, but in a field so remote,—and in which all habits of thought, feeling and expression, are so unlike, and sometimes so wholly

irreconcilable with our own,—it appeared not
undesirable to append to the Text, information
which, not disturbing the current of the narrative, might have interest for those who
would care little for an every day love-story.
Such notes may be passed over by the general reader.   There is an undoubted resemblance in the great outlines of human character
wherever man is found, but the modifications
it receives from all the varieties of climate,
education, civilization, laws and religious
usages, are worthy of a close survey; and, in
the case of China, where a far larger portion
of the human race are bound together by
similarity of language,—common traditions,—
all submitting to the same recognised authority
—all moulded to a general type,—than can be
found in any other portion of the terraqueous
globe, it is hoped that, whatever may enable us
to approach the domesticities of the Chinese
people, will not be unwelcome.

THE FLOWERY SCROLL.[1]

---

[1] The Flowery Scrolls, in China, afford an immense field for the display of the poetical, the pictorial, and the caligraphic arts. There is not a hall or great apartment, on whose pillars or walls these ornaments are wanting. They are generally suspended in pairs, and it is expected that the inscriptions should, as it were, respond to one other by comparisons, contrasts and antitheses, so that a succession of images should relieve one another by the reflection of opposed lights and shades. Here is an example in the representation of the fate of a fortunate, and an unfortunate, lover :

The bright sun rises over the eastern mountains,
A new glory re-awakens the earth to the impulses of spring ;
The pink peach flowers open their beauties to the light ;
The yellow bamboos wave, in the garden, to the gentle breezes.
He holds aloft the golden cup, and pours out its scarlet wine,
The warm wine which gives greater warmth to his warm heart.
See ! he is ascending the ladder by which he mounts to the clouds !
He approaches the condescending glance of the son of heaven !*

The watery moon has descended beneath the western valley,
The departure of the moon-goddess has filled the heaven with gloom;
The almond blossoms and fruits have all been swept away.
The fierce blast shakes the black fir-trees of the forest,
The dull, damp mists of night enshroud the earth in darkness,
And tears, frozen to ice, fall on the cold ground below.
He cannot fling down the crimson screen at the boudoir ;
His very entrails are torn with intolerable despair.†

* He has obtained the highest literary eminence, and been admitted to the Hanlin, or Doctorial College, and has obtained, in consequence, the hand of his beloved.

† Failing in his competitive examination, he has lost the favour of his lady, and the screen cannot be removed, which debars access to her apartments.

1

These scrolls serve the purposes of albums, and are often the autograph paintings, and writings of persons known to fame, or possessing the friendship of the possessor. In the " Medicine Street," at Canton, deeply engraved in blazing, golden characters, of an immense size, on a scarlet ground, was the sign-board of the principal shop in the street, being the reproduction of a scroll written by the Viceroy of Kwan Tung, Seu, who wished to convey to the physician by whom he had been cured of a serious malady, a permanent, and, as it proved to be, a very popular and a very profitable evidence of his good opinion. The literary scrolls are, for the most part, quotations from the classics ; apophthegms from the sages, and verses which have been handed down from the traditions of the past. The scrolls supply abundant and varied materials for conversation, and serve to test the acquirements of those who seek opportunities for displaying their erudition by tracing them back to their authors. It is a curious fact that, when the scent bottles, with Chinese inscriptions, were discovered at Thebes and Memphis, there was not a single instance in which we were unable to track back the verse to its original Chinese source. Commissioner Lin, the author of the Opium War, was famous for his scroll writing, the originals of which have a high money value, and fac-similes are frequently seen in Chinese houses.*

It is in this field that painters and caricaturists obtain the highest rewards, and they generally appropriate to themselves some particular department. Chang, a celebrated scroll painter of the last generation, devoted himself to the celebration of different events in the history of the sages, giving a rude, written report of the tale he has to tell, and illustrating the tale by very grotesque, but often

* I possess one of these scrolls, of which the following is a translation :—

If an upright heart be not maintained, interment in an auspicious place avails nothing :
Without filial duty to Parents, sacrifice to the Gods avails nothing :
If there be discord between brethren, harmony among friends avails nothing :
With a disorderly life, pursuit of letters avails nothing :
With a proud temper cherished, universal knowledge avails nothing :
If folly guides in the transaction of affairs, superiority of intellect avails nothing :
If the natural constitution be not attended to, to swallow medicine avails nothing :
If fate be unpropitious, wild endeavours (to gain the desired end) will avail nothing :
With the substance of others unjustly possessed, almsgiving avails nothing :
If lustful desires be entertained, piety and devotion avail nothing.

powerful painting. For example, he depictured various occurrences in the history of two slaves who were given to one of the sages by a Chinese Emperor, on condition that the sage should turn them to the very best account. He sends them to foreign lands, that they may collect specimens of fruits, flowers, and manufactures unknown, or superior to those with which his countrymen were acquainted. He makes them instruments for his moral improvement, giving to one, a red, and to the other a blue bottle, and directs the first slave to place, in the red bottle, the record of every kind and wise word that he utters, and every good deed that he performs ; while the other slave is charged to place, in the blue bottle, every foolish, or wicked word or act, and they are to bring the bottles to him at the close of every day, when, according to the instructions of the Buddhist authorities, he has to draw the balance between merits and demerits, and ascertain whether he has made a step upwards or downwards in the next stage of existence. Good hand-writing is the first requirement at all competitive examinations, and the beautiful specimens seen on the flowery scrolls, show with what success all the delicacies of that charming art are acquired. Chinese characters lend themselves to a great variety of ornaments. There are the bird—the flower—the bamboo—the vase, and other fanciful forms, to which the various signs are accommodated. Some show the minute and exquisite miniature touches of the finest pencil ; others, the bold dashing produced by brushes, such as are used for the colouring of walls, or the painting of screens and sign boards. Among the most remarkable scrolls, are those which represent the judgments of the Buddhist tribunals, after the death, and the delivery of the condemned to the devils, who are seen inflicting a variety of horrible, but appropriate tortures. There is scarcely any form of imaginable agony omitted ;—crushing to death, —sawing in two,—tearing out the peccant parts from the body with fiery pincers,—in which, all the multitudinous torments imagined by the monks of the middle ages, and exhibited in some of their convents at the present day, are out-horrified. These religious paintings form the adornment of the Buddhist temples, and are seldom seen in the private houses even of the poor. The pictorial displays found upon the scrolls are of infinite variety. Grand, historical processions,—passages of ancient history,—portraits of distinguished men and women,—pic-nic garden parties, —hunting,

hawking, fishing,—kite flying, in which the aged indulge themselves quite as much as the young ;—playing at various games, such
as draughts or chess*—love scenes, for which the Chinese novelists
and dramatists give abundant materials. In landscapes, bamboos,
forest flower trees, cascades and distant mountains are seldom
wanting. The bamboo is one of the favourite objects of Chinese
poets and painters,—and with good reason, for its uses are multitudinous as are its graces.

A very beautiful scroll, and an admirable display of Chinese art,
was given by Warren Hastings to George III., and is now in the
British Museum. It is an elaborate, almost microscopic, picture
of the City of Canton,—every temple, edifice and house, with the
factories and costumes of the nations who were then allowed to
trade. Not a vestige is left of these ancient institutions, nor, it may
be added, of those more modern fabrics.

Lin, the most distinguished of the geographers of China, a Mandarin of very high rank, sent to me a complimentary autograph scroll
in which my travels, through "sunny and snowy regions," were
illustrated by references to much legendary lore, to the writings of
distinguished Chinese statesmen and sages, and the honours they
had received from the Emperors on their return home.

The scrolls are mostly written on thin, white silk or paper, bespang-
led with gold and silver leaf. In width, from one to four feet,—in
length, they reach to the height of the pillar, or the apartment where
they are hung. They can be rolled up and fastened with silk thread,
which, being untied, the roller to which they are attached, is heavy
enough to keep them in their perpendicular position.

* The Chinese game of chess does not resemble that which has been introduced
into Europe, but is an image of their own constitution. In chess, each player has
sixteen pieces, arranged in the intersections of the lines ; the board contains seventy
two squares, divided from each other by a (broad) line, representing a river, on the
banks of which the battle is supposed to be fought. There are five pawns (common
soldiers) stationed in the van, two artillerymen (called cannons) in their rear, and
the King, with his suite of two aids (Ministers of State), two elephants, two horsemen, and two charioteers, stand in the front row. The King and his two attendant
Ministers cannot go out of the four square enclosures in which they stand, but the
subordinates can cross the river. The horsemen and charioteers correspond to our
knights and castles, but the aids, artillerymen and elephants have powers different
from any pieces in European chess. Draughts are not often played. The number of
men is 360, half of them white and half black, intended to represent the number of
days in the year.—See Dr. Williams' Middle Kingdom, ii. 91. My experience is different
I found draughts very commonly played,—but dominoes more frequently still.

CHAPTER I.

INTRODUCTION.

I STOOD leaning upon a balustrade that I might enjoy the freshness of the evening breeze. The autumnal wind wafted towards me the fragrance of the white lotus flowers, and shining like water I saw the horns of the new moon.[1] It was the very night when, as the tale is told,

---

[1] The phrase, "watery moon," is commonly used in China to betoken its want of brightness, or its waning phase. In European phraseology, "love sickness" is associated with the "pale moon," to which youths and maidens habitually address their plaints : but, in China, the "bright moon" is more intimately connected with amatory passions, as the lunar goddess possesses all the attributes attributed to the classical Diana. In truth, it has been found very convenient at once to identify the Chinese deity with her of the Pantheon, and to employ the name "Diana" as a fit representative of the Buddhist female divinity.

there is the blending of the constellations.[1] And then I thought silently that if the heavens had a happiness of their own in union and sympathy, there was no reason why man should be delivered over to sadness and solitude. If there be a day of gladness and rejoicing above, are there no jewels,—is there no fragrance for us to possess and enjoy below.[2]

Look whichever way we will—from the beginning to the end of things—love is a universal element—it always was—it always will be. The heart will follow the uncontrollable impulses of nature. It will be reckless,—dissatisfied—impatient until its affections can be mingled with the affections of another.

[1] One of the stars in Lyra, called the herdsman, (Niu Lang) is the representative of the male, and another, the webster, (Chi Niu) of the female principle. The legends call the lady the grand-daughter of Tien Ti,—the celestial ruler. She was so busily engaged in weaving embroidered stuffs, that she neglected her toilet, irritated her grandfather, who insisted on her marrying the herdsman; upon which, she abandoned her work, and Tien Ti ordered her to resume her former condition; only allowing her, once a year, on the seventh day of the seventh month, to cross the milky-way and to visit her husband. The day is made a festival for wives and maidens in China, who throw out many coloured threads, in the starlight, to honor her manufacturing industry, activity, and to condole with her short connubial felicity.

[2] "To rob precious stones,—to steal fragrance," i.e., to enjoy forbidden pleasures.

The mountains and the seas love not, yet are they linked to and attracted towards each other. How can I believe that the human race, overflowing with love, should be able to subdue its mighty influences? No! no! they are irresistible. The tides of tenderness are not to be arrested on their progress. I am about to tell you a marvellous tale.

There is a love deep as the ocean and vast as the firmament. Why should I not narrate the story for the instruction of those who come after me?

There lived in Soo Chow a clever youth whose name was Liang. His father was an Imperial functionary; his mother a most exemplary woman. He lived a lonely life, for he was brotherless. His countenance was fair as the moon,—his cheeks rosy as the spring,—his talents brilliant as new silk, or crystal clouds: yet was he gay and joyous as the man who rode triumphantly upon the whale, and as accomplished as the youth who mastered the Phœnix.[1]

Liang was eighteen years old when he was

---

[1] Li Tai Pe, a famous poet, fascinated a whale, and compelled the monster to swim with him to the celestial regions. Siaou Chi was another Chinese Orpheus, who, by the melodies of his flute, attracted

ranked among the honored list of initiated students, and he longed for the day when he might be received into the service of the Emperor.[1]

the Phœnixes to a Tower, which he had erected, and called the Phœnix Tower. One day, the musician and his wife sprung upon the back of a Phœnix and were carried away to heaven. The Phœnix of Chinese fiction is a bird, possessing every conceivable attraction: its beautiful feathers represent, in their five colours, the cardinal virtues,—its voice is melodious,—its motions graceful,—its affections full of tenderness: it has not been seen on earth in modern times, but the argus pheasant is a sort of representation of a degenerate Fung Hwang. Confucius refers to the disappearance of the Phœnix as an evidence of the downward progress of mankind.

[1] This can only be accomplished by a succession of competitive examinations. The value attached to literary distinction, not only as marking unmistakeably a man's social position, but as the stepping-stone to imperial favour, will be exemplified in the whole course of this story. There is no part of the world where education, such as it is, is so highly estimated as in China. No enquiry is made as to the rank held—the wealth or the poverty—of the successful competitor in the examination halls. In the highest grades of eminence, the student is not only himself surrounded by a halo of glory, but it is reflected on his family, his clan, and the locality of his birth. A hundred proverbs are in constant use in China, exciting youth to struggle for literary distinction as the great end and object of life. " Man's mission is as much to rise, as it is the property of water to fall." " Our primary duty is to make our family illustrious, and, by noble exertions, to bring glory to our race." " Learning will raise the lowest of the people to the highest dignities. The sons of the highest dignataries, if unlearned, are mingled with the common mass." " Ten years of study under the window (in obscurity) will bring promotion and fame under the canopy of heaven." (thro' the whole empire.) " A *Seu-Tsai* (literate), without going out of his door, is acquainted with the affairs of the whole empire." " In learning, there is neither age nor youth. The learned, whether young or old, will be raised above all."

The selection of wise and meritorious persons to high office, without any reference to their social position, is not only reported as the practice of the ancient kings, but is insisted on by Confucius, Mencius, and all the authoritative sages of China. Mencius says: "If a prince will avoid disgrace, he will honour virtue and respect the learned." "The emptiness of a country is seen when superior men are not selected to office." He thus reproved a prince: "What avails it that your kitchens overflow with costly food,—that your stables are filled with pampered horses,—if the faces of your people are pale with hunger, and their famished corpses cover your fields?" He brings forward the example of a sage, who, in the presence of one of the ancient kings, quoted two lines from the Book of Odes—

Riches and power are blessings but to those
Who soothe the widows' and the orphans' woes.

"Admirable words!" said the sovereign. "Admirable words!" and the sage answered: "If you find them admirable, why do you not practice them?" A succession of sages and censors have repeated these councils to the Emperors. As a specimen of the frankness with which the sages addressed their sovereigns, the following is an extract from a remonstrance to Ying Tsing, who ascended the throne in A. D. 1064 from Sze Ma Lung, a member of the Hanlin College, and an assistant minister of the monarch whom he had the courage thus to address: "Among the officers of your government, the good and bad are mingled and confounded,—a disorder, perilous to the State, and which your Majesty is called upon to remedy. You should ascertain who are most distinguished for virtue and capacity, and most likely to obtain the good opinion of the people. Select them from the crowd, and confer upon them the highest offices. If you live an idle life in your palace and deliver yourself over to dissolute pleasures,—if you transfer your authority to your officers, and enquire not who has merit and who has none,—if you do not distinguish between unobtrusive virtue and artfully disguised vice,—if you appoint the first candidate to place,—and, what is worse, are only influenced by your favoritism or your resentment,—if you banish those who have displeased, and promote those who flatter you,—if you use your power to reward sycophants and to punish honest advisers, whose sincerity is their only crime, you will have confusion both in your court and your country;—no more law,—no more order,—no more peace. Can anything be more dangerous to the Empire and to yourself?"

CHAPTER II.

LIANG TAKES LEAVE OF HIS MOTHER AND ENTERS UPON HIS TRAVELS.

IT was in a calm and pleasant mood that Liang strolled into the flower garden, whose atmosphere seemed unusually sweet and grateful. Many tame birds were playing among the branches, and they, too, joined their thrilling songs with the fresh fragrance that welcomed the wanderer. Yet a certain melancholy oppressed him as he saw leaf by leaf of the peach-bloom fall into the water below and the leaves were carried off by the stream.[1] They were

[1] Peach trees have a sort of sacredness among the Chinese. Peaches are symbols of long life or immortality. They are constantly introduced into paintings and sculptures, and are considered

whirled about by the breezes as they fell, for the spring was departing, and they taught the lesson that, all which concerns humanity is changeful as the winds and the clouds.[1]   All is vanity that is not linked with enjoyment.   The almond blossoms that drop into the water are borne about by its eddies, they meet, they part, and are all swept away.   Yet, whether lingering in the ponds, or carried away by the running stream, they are attracted towards one another, moved by a common sympathy, unwilling to journey alone.   "And I have passed," thought he, "eighteen years in useless study, —in loneliness unloving.   This must not be.

as appropriate presents to superiors. The ancient books are full of testimonies to the virtues of the peach. There is a peach tree on the Kwoh Mountain which only produces one fruit in a thousand years, and he who eats it will never die. Another is celebrated in the Taouist Legends, which grew 3,000 years before it blossomed, and 3,000 years more before the blossoms ripened into fruit. There was also a peach of death which always bore two kernels; it was of ravishing beauty, but a deadly poison. Another peach tree is said to have sheltered hundreds of demons, who concocted under its shadow their schemes for doing mischief to mankind. The secret society of the Hung pledges its members to fealty under peach trees. —See *Memoires concernant les Chinois.*

[1] An ancient Chinese aphorism says : "As the winds and clouds of heaven are ever shifting, so the misery and happiness of men change from morning to evening,"—meaning that the fortunes of mankind fluctuate as the winds and the clouds.

Is there no Tsin Ying in the world, to care
for me, to instruct me, to lead me into the
western pavilion.[1]   I have heard that Chang
Chow is renowned for its beauties fair and
rosy, soft and charming, each vieing with the
others in the graces of their toilettes.   I will
take up my abode there; there will I look
for happiness."   He danced about the hall, delighted with the resolution he had taken.   He
hastened to his mother, and said: "I cannot
pursue my studies here.   I have no friends
to aid me.   What can I do alone?   I have
heard that in Chang Chow there are multitudes of learned men, and that it is easy to get
introductions to the very best society.   I must
learn from the learned.[2]   I must dispute with

[1] Tsin Ying is a heroine of Chinese novels,—the model of womanly
grace and virtue. She encouraged the studies of Chang, her lover.
Her life was full of vicissitude, but all the stories report the success,
in the competitive examinations, of him to whom she was attached.
The western pavilion is sometimes called the Palace of the Moon, to
reach which, a magician made of his conjuring stick a bridge from
earth to heaven. He conducted the Emperor Ming over the bridge
to the palace, where he found a beautiful nymph, of whom he became
enamoured. Returning to earth, he built an edifice resembling
that which he had visited, and in inviting the goddess to adorn it,
was informed that, when he could draw the moon out of the water
his wish would be fulfilled.

[2] A diligent perseverance in the pursuit of literary fame is con-

the doctors. I have come to tell you of my purpose, and to say to you Good-bye!" "Treasure of a son," she answered, "I have heard that a student always wants the help of fellow-students. And I remember we have an aunt in Chang Chow. Her name is Yao. She is dying for news of us, and what luck! to-morrow is the anniversary of her birth. You shall go with our birthday gifts; you shall take our congratulations.[1] She will offer you

---

stantly inculcated. "Determine to do it, and the deed is done!" says one apophthegm. Another: "Waste not your time like the fisherman who fishes for three days, and then throws away two in drying his nets." Again, "The resolution which begins with youth, will bring honour to age." And, again, "He who is old cannot replace the studies which he neglected when young."

[1] Birth-day gifts in every shape, and congratulations more or less formal, according to the relative position of the parties are associated with these anniversaries. As the Chinese have no regular days of rest, labour is continuous, except on the various festivals of the gods, or at the commencement of the year, when the holidays last for many days. The ceremonial visits are accompanied with various observances. Guests are formally announced, who always come in choice apparel, and are received with bows and prostrations, and congratulations of the most exaggerated character, each professing the greatest self-humility and the highest respect for the other. Inquiries are made into the health and well-doing of all the members of the family, and sweetmeats, cakes and other aliments, with tea and wine, are prepared for the guests. They are preceded by large crimson cards, so that preparations may be made for their becoming reception. The form of announcement on a visiting card is, "Your stupid younger brother bows his head to salute you." If the

you an apartment. She will take care of you.
She will find you a meet companion. The
olive branch of the moon[1] is not so far away.
You shall win the competitive prize. You
shall crown the family with honour and glory.
I am only sorry your father is absent, and that
he cannot at once take charge of the family

person is requested to enter, the words of reception are: " How can
I presume to receive the honourable footsteps that have taken this
trouble. Is it well with the gentleman in the chariot?" If there
be a student in the family of the visitor, the topic becomes prominent. "He will perpetuate the fragrance of literature,"—to which
the appropriate reply is, "Happiness is poor in hills and fields."
(*i.e.*, we have no great reputation). It is a matter of politeness to
avoid mentioning names or parentage, except by a periphrase.
"Does the honourable, great man enjoy felicity?" for, "Is your
father well?" "Illustrious and venerable one, what honorable age?"
for "How old is he?" The father of the host is called by the guest
"The sire of the house." "The excellent and honourable." "The
venerable, great prince." A son speaks of his father as "family's
majesty,"—of a dead mother, as "the venerable great one who is at
rest." The mistress of the house is enquired for as "the excellent
longevity hall." If a man have but one son, he answers to the inter-
rogation as to the number of "excellent young gentlemen in his family?"—"Mine is a niggardly fate, I have only one little bug." A
man calls his own wife "The mean one inside," or the "family
foolish one," while every grandiose phrase is used by a visitor to
his host.—See Bridgman's "Chinese Chrestomathia," a treasury of
useful information for a student of Chinese.

[1] When the Emperor Ming was conducted to the Palace of the
Moon, he found an olive tree, in remembrance of which he planted
one in his own "Western Pavilion;" and when a student obtains the
highest honour, a branch of the olive tree is presented to him.

affairs. Never mind. Dear, dearest boy! Go. Go, and come back, for if you come not back I shall destroy myself.[1] I cannot bear the thought of not seeing you again."

Liang bowed reverently, and said "Fare-well!" The servants busied themselves in packing up his belongings, in collecting the birthday presents, and he embarked on the river Chang.

---

[1] Suicides are so common in China that they excite little atten-tion. They often terminate unfortunate love affairs. Opium is generally the instrument of death; but among the aristocratical classes, the eating of gold-leaf is considered a more dignified mode of self-destruction. I remember one of our servants quietly re-porting that his wife had hanged herself that morning; he said it was very improper, for she had chosen a day when he was particu-larly busy. It will be seen throughout our story how frequently the principal actors speak of the sacrifice of their lives. It may be said that in China life is held to be of little value, man's mundane existence being but a fragment of his many-staged being. A substi-tution is allowed for many offences in China; and where the law is satisfied with life for life, there is likely difficulty in finding candidates for capital punishment, whose ordinary market price is a hundred ounces of silver, about £30 sterling.

CHAPTER III.

LIANG PRESENTS THE FAMILY CONGRATULATIONS
TO LADY LAO.

LIANG bade the boatmen to be diligent, and swiftly the boat sped over the blue water. The songs of the rowers mounted to the heavens, and the hawks floated above their heads.

They anchored at Soo Chow, and, at the city walls,[1] he left the boat to seek the Lady Yao.

[1] The passage boats which ply on the canals and rivers in China, usually convey their passengers to the walls of the towns and cities, which they enter under arched bridges, through narrow inlets, that can at any time be closed against them. Almost all travel is undertaken by water, as the roads are few, bad and narrow. Wheeled carriages are almost unknown, except in the capital, and even those who are conveyed in sedan chairs have often to cross the rice-fields in which an elevated path is generally left for the convenience of wayfarers. The few horses that are seen are of wretched breeds and wretchedly cared for. Goods are generally carried on men's shoulders, suspended at the ends of plastic stems of bamboo, whose elasticity relieves the bearer of a portion of the dead weight.

His servants preceded him with the crimson cards which bore his name, and announced his arrival. They returned from the ante-hall and brought greetings of welcome from the lady, requesting the immediate presence of her nephew, who entered, made a low bow,[1] and said, as he approached his aunt, " My mother has charged me to present her respectful salutations and best wishes : she hopes you will con· descend to accept some worthless gifts. Deign to receive them as evidence, too, of the warmth of my affection." On looking at the presents, Lady Yao was delighted. She bestowed upon him her most gracious smile. " I hope that your

---

[1] There are eight degrees of reverence laid down by the Chinese authorities, whose observance is made peremptory by law. The first and lowest and commonest form of salutation is when the hands are joined and raised before the breast.' This is the *Kung Shau.* In the second, the *Tso Yih*, a low bow accompanies the raising the hands. The third, the *Ta Tsien*, requires the knees to be bent as if about to kneel. The *Kwei*, or fourth, is actual kneeling. The fifth is the *Ko Tau*, which was the subject of so many controversies when· exacted from foreigners at court, where there is kneeling and knocking the head. In the sixth, *San Kau*, the head is three times knocked. In the seventh, *Luh Kau*, there is kneeling and knocking thrice, then standing up, and again there is kneeling and knocking. The culminating climax is the *San Kwei Kiu Kau*, where there are three distinct kneelings and nine knockings of the head.—*William's Mid. King.*, ii., 68, 69.

virtuous mother is happy, and that your honored
father is well and prosperous. We will take
care of your comforts, worthy nephew! There
are still some fragrant olive branches in the
palace of the moon![1]   I am very, very thankful
for your liberal presents. I shall remember.
I shall not forget them!" "You are much too
good," answered Liang, "They are undeserving
of your kind notice. I was quite ashamed to
present them. My mother enjoys health and
peace. Your stupid nephew has no merits to
enable him to bring honour to the family. In

[1] An obscure hint that old Lady Lao would interest herself in
any matrimonial arrangements on behalf of her nephew. She is
quite alive to the bright prospects which his literary talents promised. To mention the moon and olive branches in the same sen-
tence, was a pretty way of suggesting that the youth might be
looking round for an appropriate partner. It may be seen throughout this novel, that in China the great object of men is to obtain
literary distinction, and of parents to provide literary alliances for
their daughters. An ancient axiom is often cited :—

"In choosing a husband for your daughter, take care that he is
superior to her in rank, that she may serve him with becoming respect and reverence,—in choosing a wife for yourself, let her be your
inferior, that she may bring becoming services to your family." Of
women in China, among the higher ranks, it may be truly said with
Byron, " Love is their sole existence,"

> "For all of them upon that die is thrown,
> And if 'tis lost, life hath no more to bring
> To them, but mockeries of the past alone."

our humble abode there was no talented man
to help him. To remain there would have driven
him to despair; but he had heard that there
were many distinguished men in your illustrious city, and perhaps among them he might
find a friend and a master, and with his, and your
gracious patronage, he might look upward."
Lady Yao smiled a most benignant approval.
" Listen, my dear Mr. Liang! I know that your
literary acquirements are very great, and great
distinctions await you. A day may come when
your name will be recorded in the Jasper
Hall.[1] Do not complain of the shabbiness of
my poor abode, but remain among us and pursue your studies." Liang again bowed most
reverentially. "How can I sufficiently thank
your great goodness? I shall never forget
your indulgent reception, and gracious offer of
an apartment," he continued. " And may I
still further intrude, and venture to ask to be
introduced to my cousin, that our present
meeting may sweeten the sorrows of our long
separation?" The Lady Lao responded: " My
honoured Lord Lao, I hear, has been advanced

---

[1] The Hanlin, or Doctorial College.

to the rank of Major-General. My son is occupied, reading in his study. He has been arranging his books, and how glad I am that you, my dearest nephew, are come to study with him. You will give light to the stupid blindness of my son."[1] The Lady despatched a servant to summon the young student to her presence. He came with the speediest obedience to the inner chamber. The cousins were de- lighted to meet one another. Wine was brought in, and each pledged the other with hearty salutations. Each was ready to encourage each. They filled their glasses, and filled them again. Truth to say, they drank far too much; the cheeks of both were crimson as peaches; and each announced to the other that the moon was shining for him in the Western Pavilion.

---

[1] In intercourse, personal or epistolary, the Chinese use the most exaggerated expressions, in deprecation of themselves and their be- longings, and of laudation of the persons and possessions of those they address. Their own abodes, however grand, they call their " humble cottage,"—that, however lowly of him with whom they converse, "the illustrious palace." Evidences of this extravagant form of expression pervade this and all Chinese novels.

CHAPTER IV.

CONFIDENCES BETWEEN THE TWO COUSINS.

AFTER making the becoming reverences to Lady Yao, the two students walked towards the study apartments. They took one another by the hand[1] and danced around the enclosure. On one side was a rambling path, bordered with bamboos. They walked by the ponds with the golden fish, and peeped into the conservatories. A servant had placed wax lights in their sockets, and immediately after entering the room, they sat down on their heels in the chair, lifted up their knees to their chins,[2] and began the usual

---

[1] It is a custom for friends to walk holding each other's hand.

[2] A common posture among the Chinese, who frequently sit upon chairs, as other orientals sit on the ground, with their knees propping up their chins.

gossip about the moon and the weather, when the moonlight entered the window. Lao rose up, and said to Liang, " Cousin of mine! your body interrupts the entrance of the moonshine; the shadow of the flowers is upon the grating, and, according to my notion, no one who sees the moon and the flowers together can be ungrateful for the return of spring. It is said, some people are so restless that they are always travelling hither and thither. Why should they be so weary of the business of life?" Liang smiled, and answered, "Brother, brother! you are not sensitive enough. Who is there that does not enjoy the zephyrs and the moonlight, and who likes to abandon his own old homestead? but men are ever fascinated by the pursuit of fame and glory, in search of which they eat the wind and sleep upon the sea."

They were thus discoursing, when Lady Yao sent a message for her son. He saluted his cousin, departed for the great hall, and Liang was left alone in the study.

CHAPTER V.

PLAYING AT DRAUGHTS.

LIANG saw nothing but books; row over row upon the shelves. The room was circled with pots of flowers, which filled it with their odours. On the table was a lute, upon a jade stand, and clouds of fragrant smoke rose from a golden hafing dish. A silver harpsichord, and a lute of jasper hung upon the walls. In a corner were two draught-boards, and, on both sides, scrolls of ancient poetry and fanciful paintings, representing lakes and woods, and bridges and pagodas. The scrolls were suspended in pairs. He stood up to feel the fresh air from the window, looking upon a winding balustrade which hung over a white lotus, that was swimming on the lake below. A stork crept slowly and stealthily along in the moonlight; the wind shook down the willow catkins upon the water, over which, a vermilion painted bridge led to the inner garden. He admired the stripes of wavelets, broken by the light of the moon. On both banks, the branches of mournful willows were trembling, under one of which a boat was fastened, to enable the gardener to attend to the lotus flowers.[1] Gold fish, bright as satin in the sun, darted through the ponds, on whose surface the cloud-shadows were reflected. Liang crossed the bridge, and entered a pavilion on the farther side. From the balustrade he stretched his hand to gather a rose, the branch broke, and the frightened birds flew away. A

[1] The lotus is a singularly beautiful flower, and is much attended to in the fish-ponds, which are among the constant ornaments of Chinese gardens. It has been not unaptly called "the child of the sun," as it comes to the surface to welcome the sunrise, and hides itself under the water when the sun descends. Its stem is four or five feet long, supporting an elegantly formed cup, about eight inches in diameter, formed of soft white leaves, delicately pencilled with rosy stripes, having fruit in the centre, an inverted cone of bright green encircled by a fringe of golden anthers. The Hung Hwui, the secret society which overruns China, whose purpose is to restore the Ming dynasty, and is intimately connected with the Taeping and other insurrectionary movements, has made the lotus one of its sacred symbols. The place of their assemblages is called the Blue Lotus Hall.—*Hung League, Schlegel's Introduc.*, p. xxxv.

cuckoo cried as if it were the waning of the moon.

The piping of the ·goldfinches troubled his spirits; their flight interfered with the moon-beams. Drops of dew hung upon the flowers. He passed another small bridge and came on a slippery path, on which unripe plums were lying. Two peacocks strutted away, and a cockatoo screamed from a golden cage.[1] Before him, was a park, wrapt in the shadows of spring. Two lines of peach trees formed a charming alley. " Surely this is a fit abode for spirits," whispered Liang to himself. " Would that the fisherman were here!"[2] Proceeding westward, he crossed a garden of red apricot trees: he admired their bloom, and passed over turfs of luxurious and sweet-smelling grass, from which climbing rose trees sprung, and inter-

[1] All these were evil omens. A Chinese superstition declares that the cuckoo's note is never heard till the moon is on the wane; the waning of the moon and the obstruction of its rays are associated with sorrow and disappointment. Dew drops represent the tears of the flowers.

[2] Sir John Davis gives the legend of the fisherman who followed some peach blossoms, driven by the wind to a narrow creek, which he crossed, and found a race of men living in primitive innocence, having no intercourse with the outer world. He returned home,— narrated what he had seen, but never again was able to find the lost paradise.

twined themselves in mulberry branches. He did not linger long among these attractive scenes, but returned with slow steps to the study.

The night was advancing, and he was surprised when sounds from a distant draught-board met his ear. " Who, at this late hour, can be so busy at play ? " With the softest tread, he approached the eastern side, and saw in the distance a tub with peonies. Half shaded by the trees, he perceived a lighted lamp, and under the trees several persons were seated. He heard bursts of laughter, with which the voices of girls were mingled. The air was burthened with the scent of fragrant flowers. He stole stealthily to a spot, whence, unobserved, he might spy what was going on. The moon was overclouded, so that, even if discovered, the female servants would take him for the young Lao, and nothing would be reported by them to their mistresses. Liang returned to the stone balustrade, and saw two lovely, graceful ladies, laughing together and playing at draughts.

The long hair of the lady who sat on the western side was hanging loosely over her shoulders. At the first glance, Liang's heart was overwhelmed. "This is no common wo-man," he said, "she resembles one of the nymphs by whom Lin Lang was allured."[1] His presumption broke all bounds. He flung off his outer garments, and sprang forward to salute the ladies. Little dreamed he of the fright he caused. They closed their glittering eyes. Meanwhile, another youth was seen approach-ing. They let the draught-board fall, and fled. But, while they fled, he took emphatic note of their persons. The expression of their coun-tenances was that of the Fu Yung;[2] their eye-brows, long willow leaves; their red lips, most charming and alluring;—in a word, their form and features were perfect, enough to transpierce the heart of any man.[3] He heard their silken

[1] Lin Lang and a friend, when wandering among the mountains in search of medicinal plants, came to a ferry, which two maidens, of super-human beauty, invited them to cross, and conducted them to a grotto, in which they passed many blissful years. At last, desiring to revisit their native home, the nymphs allowed them to return. They found their children's children, down to the seventh generation. So long had their absence lasted,—so rapidly the time of that absence had fled.

[2] Hibiscus mutabilis.

[3] A well-known description of a beautiful Chinese woman is: " Almond-flower cheeks,—peach-blossom lips,—willow leaf waist,— bright-dancing ripple-eyes,—lotus-flower footsteps."

garments fluttering in the wind; he saw their noiseless golden lilies,[1] not two inches long, disappear. Once they looked round, and he perceived a smile upon their cheeks.

" Under these trees will I die! "[2] exclaimed Liang.

[1] Small feet.

[2] The small value attached to life, and the unconcern with which the Chinese die, or contemplate death, may be attributed to two causes,—the belief in predestination, and in the metempsychosis : the first, teaching that it is in vain to struggle against what is inevitable ; the second, that our mortal stage of being, is but a fragment of our whole and interminable existence, to another phase of which death conducts us. The fact (mentioned before) that a man can be bought in the market for about 100 ounces of fine silver, to be publicly executed for another, is associated with the opinion, that such self-sacrifice is not only a merit to be rewarded hereafter, but has its recompense here in enabling the victim to make provision for his family, and the deed will be recorded as honourable on the Tablet of the ancestral hall. The French Ambassador informed me that the Elders of a Chinese village were astonished when he refused to accept two old men for sacrifice, in exchange for a young man who had been condemned to death for assaulting a Frenchman. On one occasion, when I had to complain to the Governor of Kiang Su, of the misconduct of some Chinese soldiers, we found six men kneeling, —who were perfectly innocent,—and His Excellency offered, as a becoming expiation, to behead them in the presence of myself and the Admiral who accompanied me. I have seen a corpse lying under the gambling tables at Canton, and I once stumbled over the dead body of a man when entering the door of an American missionary : neither the authorities nor passengers concerned themselves in the least about so common an occurrence,—so have I frequently noticed old and decrepid people abandoned to starve and die on the highways, when the basin of rice, placed by their side, was exhausted.

Meanwhile, the serving maidens followed their mistresses. Liang reeled against the balcony like a drunken man. The sisters took one another by the hand, and, without uttering a word, returned to their odoriferous boudoir.

Infanticide is justified by Chinese moralists, who teach that it is better the infant should suffer the pain of a moment, by drowning or strangling, than that it should live a life of misery and crime. I have seen ponds, into which "toothless children," generally females, are thrown,—and mothers frequently prefer destroying their offspring, to delivering them over to the tender mercies of orphan asylums, which are not wanting in the great cities. I remember an argument used,—and it was deemed the most satisfactory against infanticide : "If your mothers had committed such a deed, where would you have been?"—but the sinfulness of the act is not, as far as I remember, denounced by any high authority.

Indifference to death,—and the sacrifice of life on the slightest occasions, are every day witnessed in China. I once saw twenty men executed, and though close by, I did not hear a word uttered, or observe the slightest resistance, when the executioners arranged their bodies to receive the fatal blow.

CHAPTER VI.

PI YUE SAYS NOTHING ABOUT THE GAME OF DRAUGHTS.

WHEN the lovely ladies had seated themselves, the young lady Yao enquired of Yun Liang: "What were your people doing, to make that young man on the balustrade reel to and fro? I never saw him before. I am ill at ease, lest he should have seen my unveiled face. I wonder to what family he belongs; his rashness is no great recommendation!" Yun Liang, who had listened very attentively, thus replied. "My Lady! kindly hear me. Your unworthy maidens were standing among the flowers. The moon was clouded over, and it was impossible to recognise anybody. Everyone said it was young

Yao, but, whoever it was, really the youth's manners were not amiss." And Miss Tsai Ki rejoined: "When I was walking with my slave girls, I heard a whisper that Liang had arrived. It was said that our honourable aunt had kindly received him; had offered him a bed in the student-chamber; had given him wine to drink. And I thought that, perhaps, after drinking, he might have gone to refresh himself in the moonlight. Was there anything improper in his wandering among the flowers?" Miss Yao suddenly said to the maid servant, Pi Yue: "Did you not leave the draughts scattered upon the terrace? Now, I dare say, Liang is returned home. Do you go and gather the draughts together, but mind you come back soon, —very soon." Pi Yue replied that she would most reverently obey her Lady's commands, and off she went hurriedly; but she walked very slowly through the flower-garden,—she lingered long under the willow trees,—she took a round about the fish-pond,—and, at last, she discovered that Liang had not departed. He was leaning on the balustrade like a demented man; his cheeks were burning red, and his two hands supported his chin. He looked stupid and silent. "I wonder," said she to herself, "whether he is enamoured. Is he troubled with the thoughts of some fair damsel? Why, there are a thousand pretty, fascinating girls in the world. I should like to know how many men there are dying of unrequited love, whom the smile of a maiden might bring to life!" And so she drew near to the peony tub. Liang saw her, and bowed his body low; his soul had fled to a fair maiden. "Can this visit have a meaning for me? Clouds and rain"[1] he said to himself: then, loud enough to be heard by Pi Yue, "What lady was that clad in pure white garments? Had she descended from the western pavilion? or was she an angel from Paradise[2] itself? O, whenever she takes her homeward, heavenward way, she will carry my soul with her. Would she, before her departure, grant

---

[1] The Emperor Siang, being tired, fell asleep in the sunshine, and dreamt that he was visited by a woman of celestial beauty. He asked whence she came and who she was? " I live on the terrace of the Sun, in the Énchanted Mountain. In the morning I am a cloud, in the evening a shower of rain." Hence, the Chinese give, to the hidden sympathies of lovers, the name of " clouds and rain-showers."

[2] Pung Lai, the abode of the blessed.

me one look from her bright eyes,—favour me with one smile from her sweet lips —thought of ecstacy! What good fortune would it not be! Will you, my pretty girl, do me the kind service which was done to the student, Chang, when he courted the fair Tsui? Will you have the goodness to take charge of a letter for me?" "Impudent fellow!" exclaimed Pi Yue. ' 'When you shall resemble him, whom the maiden of the Western Pavilion loved, you may find a letter-bearer to the chaste presence. But let me counsel you, young man! Avoid these impassioned outbreaks. The laws that regulate household intimacies are cold as ice. The proprieties must not be neglected, Sir! We must not be climbing the peach trees in order to reach the clouds, nor be hungering by the side of the apricot that is nearest the sun. Better return home, take a flaming sword, cut your love fancies into bits, and find rest for your soul." And she sprang upon the terrace, gathering up the draughts one by one. Liang laughed out, and said, " You say well, Miss! The princess must not be sullied; but why exhibit to me all her grace and loveliness? Every-

thing about her was good humoured and charming; and did she not laugh again and again?
Now, cannot you find out for me a way to
heaven, and help me to convey a certain lady
into the golden pavilion?[1]   Will not you lead
us over the azure bridge.[2]?   I will never, never
forget your goodness,—never, never be ungrateful!" Pi Yue answered: "They who do
not love, know nothing about love.   If my
mistresses laughed, it was at your ignorance of
all the proprieties.[3]   You let your tongue too

---

[1] The abode of Tsui, otherwise named Hung, the Chinese Goddess
of Chastity.

[2] The azure bridge is described by a Chinese poet as being the
grotto of the fairies, through which we must pass to a rough road
which conducts to the Jasper City.

[3] These "proprieties" or "decorums" cover the whole field of virtue in the Chinese mind.   The *Tao Li* represents and comprehends the
entire moral and ceremonial code.   "He who practices the Tao Li,"
says one of the great authorities, "will properly discharge every
duty which he owes to his family at home, and to society abroad."
The term has been translated by "The thorough understanding of
the rights of things." *Tao* means whatever is reasonable and proper,
Li, moral and ritual observances.   The Taoist creed as taught by its
founder Lao Tze, makes Reason the ground-work of the whole system.   The title of the late Emperor was *Tao Kwang*, or Reason's
Light.   In conversation, an appeal to Tao Li settles all questions of
right or wrong.   Whatever is accordant with Tao Li, is innocent, if
not meritorious; whatever is condemned by Tao Li is indefensible.

Though the educated and higher classes would alone hold themselves
as warranted to decide whether, in a particular case, the require-

loose, and my ladies will not open their ears to the out-pourings of your mouth." And so

ments of Tao Li had been carried out, the very lowest among the Chinese would admit the Tao Li authority. Right and wrong, among us, are very rude, but emphatic terms for conveying approval or disapproval. Apart, however, from what we call the moral or the religious field, there is, in China, a field, which we may denominate the Ceremonial, which is of the highest national importance, and whose influence is deeply engraved in the national character. The Board of Ceremonies, in Peking, is of equal authority with the other Boards which represent the great departments of Government. It is, in fact, the expounder of the Tao Li text,—and it is not difficult to see that Reason and Courtesy might serve as a very broad foundation for raising upon them the superstructure of a tolerably perfect legislation with its rewards and punishments. *Li* is used by Confucius in a very extensive sense. He says : " In the height of joy, *Li* teaches moderation ; in the depths of mourning it moderates grief." Again, " without *Li*, respect becomes a painful load,—without *Li*, prudence is changed into timidity,—without *Li*, courage becomes insubordination,—without *Li*, frankness will become folly." In Dr. Marshman's Translations, he frequently uses *Reason* as the proper rendering of the word,—but in its all-embracing character it is untranslatable. When Commissioner Yeh, a great classical authority, and a Member of the Hanlin College, who was constantly in the habit of referring to the *Tao Li*, as the beginning and end of the moral code, was asked to define the exact meaning of the words, he answered, " *Tao Li* is the same thing as *Tien Ming*, the ' celestial will,'—and being pressed to give an interpretation of *Tien Ming*, he said it was ' the same thing as *Tao Li*.' "

He was one day induced to expatiate on the future destiny of a man who had made the *Tao Li* the guide of his conduct. " Such a one," he said, " if he did not become a perfect man, would approach perfection, and after his mortal career is closed, be transformed to a *Shen*, or spirit, occupying a higher or a lower degree, according to his merits, and enjoying the sort of deification with which Confucius, Mencius, and other great sages have been honoured. At

she went away laughing.　Liang remained bewildered in the garden. "I have said nothing indecorous," he bethought himself, "but how shall I ever get over the perplexities and vexations which this night has brought to me."

the end of his earthly existsnce, his merits and his demerits will be weighed against each other, and if the result is unsatisfactory, another lease of existence will be allotted to him, at the termination of which, the same test will be applied, and if, then, the result of the comparison of the aggregate of virtue and vice be condemnatory, a third experimental existence would be allotted to him, and if, at last, on the whole survey, the case should show that the discipline of three lives had failed to reform, the sinner would be delivered over to one of the judges, who preside over the nine hells for final punishment.

CHAPTER VII.

FOOLISH DREAMS OF STUDENT LIANG.

His eyes followed the pretty girl, who hastily glided away, but he saw the moon's rays, sloping through the willow branches, reflected upon her silken dress; bordering the milky-way were a few scattered stars. It seemed to him that the flowers had lost their evening odours, and the place was filled with intolerable gloom. Slowly he made his way—it appeared both long and dreary—towards the study, where he called to mind his former conversation with his cousin.

"Ought any man to murmur who has the moonbeams and the flowers around him? Yet how can I deliver myself from my embarrassments? Have I used the proper means for healing a torn heart? Have I not been led astray by a seducer? What care I if I die among the flowers?"

So musing, he entered the study. He lay down but he could not sleep through the whole night. His heart was hungering and thirsting after that lovely girl, whose graceful form he had seen in the light of the lamp. "How beautiful she was! how superior was her toilette to that of ordinary women! Her hair was ornamented with a single chloranthus flower,[1]—her dress of white muslin covered with a silken robe.[2]

---

[1] The Chloranthus inconspicuus is a fragrant flower, common in Japan and China, and thought to be "love exciting." Its Chinese name is *Chu Lan*. It was believed to be used for scenting tea, and has been confounded with the Aglaia odorata, which is called *Yu Chu Lan.—Fortune's Residence in China*, p. 201.

The Chloranthus is sometimes called the Kin Lan, or golden orchid. In the classic *Y King*, or Book of Changes, attributed to Confucius, it is said, "Words of sympathy are fragrant like the Chloranthus." There is a volume entitled the Golden Orchid Book, which treats of love and friendship ; and the phrase, "golden orchid," or "Chloranthus covenant," is equivalent to the swearing an oath of everlasting amity.—See *Schlegel's Hung*, p. 20.

[2] The use of silk garments, in China, dates from the highest antiquity, and the cultivation of the Mulberry Tree is often the subject of Imperial decrees. Confucius says: "A head dress of fine cloth, it was formerly the custom to wear. Now, head dresses are made of silk. It is less costly, and I will imitate the less costly example

Her outer garment just reached her knees. How gracefully did her delicate fingers handle the draughts! Wonder not that my heart is agitated. I believe that little image of Buddha[1] is thinking of her. The lady, clad in black, who sat on the northern side, was very pretty, but not to be compared with my lady-love, who was clad in white. Since I saw her among the flowers, I feel as if my being was cemented with hers, and I grieve that I cannot fly to her, —that I cannot approach her."

of the multitude." It was deemed a reproach to any man, who, having passed the middle period of life, had been unable, by his economies, to provide himself silken robes, to be used for all festivals and holidays. There are several pretty proverbs associated with the food and the produce of the silk-worm. "A splendid silk garment is hidden in the mulberry leaf." "He who would wear robes of silk should plant the mulberry tree."

[1] Images of Buddha are everywhere seen and commonly addressed on occasions of perplexity. They are supposed to sympathise with human griefs, and to provide means of consolation. I remember once in my wanderings in China to have penetrated into a wood, in one of whose deepest recesses a small image of Buddha was placed in a little cavity of a granite rock. A poor woman was kneeling before it, and she kindled a small taper, and from time to time lighted an incense stick, which she placed before the image. The first expression of her countenance was full of agony, but soon a smile came over her face, and it was obvious she felt that she had obtained an auspicious answer to her prayers. I believe the Chinese fancy not that the idol itself is enabled to comply with the supplications of the worshipper, but that it serves as intercessor or mediator with some unseen mysterious influence greater than itself which disposes of men's destinies.

He heard the roll of the watch drum.[1] The moon and the stars were set, and the many coloured clouds of the morning were seen in the east.

---

[1] The beating of the drum, in China, like the call of the Muezzims from the Minarets, among the Mussulmans " to prayer," is often referred to as one of the mementos of duty to be done. One of the sages says : " I am summoned by the drum to remember my responsibilities to the Court, and I follow thee, my friend! in thy aspirations for public honours, I think of the place of thy birth, and watch thy footsteps in the career of promotion."

CHAPTER VIII.

STUDENT LIANG INTERROGATES HIS AUNT.

THE red orb rose out of the orient, but the sadness of the student dwelt with him till the full dawn of day. He languidly combed and washed himself, and with slow tread walked up and down the apartment. The old lady had risen early, and seated in the reception hall, she sent for the student, and thus addressed him: " Good Nephew! the days must seem long in your airy study, with nothing to do: but, do you know, there is a bridge, over which you can pass to the inner garden, where you will find plenty of flowers and singing birds, and pretty landscapes. Now, when you are weary of repeating poetry and reading books, and you want a little recreation for your tired spirit, you should take a walk thither, and get rid of your dejection."

It was a fine opportunity for unbosoming his thoughts, and Liang said: "Yestereven I enjoyed the fragrance of a hundred varieties of beautiful flowers. The landscape was lovely as that of the abode of the blessed. It enchanted those who looked on; it made them forgetful even of their own dear homes.[1] I came accidentally upon the peony tubs, and saw there two lovely ladies, laughing and playing at draughts. I wonder what their names might be."

"O!" answered Lady Yao, with a smile: "O, they were the daughters of your uncle. They came here with congratulations on the anniversary of my birthday.[2] The name of the

---

[1] The love of the Chinese for their ancestral homes is a part of their national religion. Not to be gathered to the graves of their forefathers is a grievous misery, and even a disgrace. The wandering spirits who cannot find a resting place with their progenitors, are held to be the most wretched of the wretched dead. Hundreds of coffins are brought to China from distant countries, that the corpses may be interred in the family grave.

[2] There are volumes prescribing "the proprieties" as applied to all the relations of society and the events of life. One of the ancient forms of birthday greeting, was: "I welcome the day of thy birth. I drink to thy health in wine. I supplicate for thee the three benedictions."—(Riches—Longevity—Male children.)

one with the short hair is Ma. Her mother is my sister. Her pre-name is Tsai ki, and she is fifteen years old. She is a charming person, very intelligent, far, far above the common race of girls. We settled yesterday, at the festival, that she should be betrothed to my son. The one whose hair hangs over her shoulders is my brother's daughter. She has a strange, but, perhaps, natural fancy for white garments. That is Yao Sien, the cousin of the other; her family name is Yang. She writes beautiful verses,— she sings them more beautifully still; everybody is enchanted with her. Then she plays on the lute. She knows everything, and knows everything perfectly. According to my belief, there is not so charming a girl in the whole province.[1] She does not belong to the second rank. I have measured her golden lilies,—they are not two inches long."

Was not this enough to agitate poor Liang's heart? Heart, indeed, he had none; his heart had been transferred to the maiden's elegant boudoir, his body only was in the hall. He looked stupefied. Lady Yao put several ques-

[1] Chastity in thought—purity in speech—beauty in person, and talent for embroidery, constitute the virtues of woman, according to the Chinese axiom.

tions to him.   He stammered and stammered, but made no intelligible reply.

My Lady ordered wines[1] to be brought to the water-lily pavilion, and asked the student to walk with her into the fresh air.   At her command, he took up the golden goblet, sat himself down sadly by the portal, but found neither freshness nor fragrance in the breeze.   Where was the divine maiden of yesternight?   Lady Yao half guessed at what was passing in his mind.   She told an attendant to bring the old drinking horn, and said to the student, with a smile: "They say that study can bring odour from the moon.   Chang Ngo[2] has ever loved young people.   Nephew of mine!   She has her eyes on you, and when you enter the Western Pavilion she will be your mediator; she will find for you a beautiful and becoming partner."   Liang soon discovered her meaning; his countenance brightened,—he seized the sparkling cup,—he emptied it to the very last drop.

[1] As, in the case of teas, all sorts of fanciful and flowery names are given to wines.   Among them, "the scarlet literary forest," in honour of the Hanlin College,—the "inflammable Fan Shu, or sweet potato.—"Red twelve Cash," a name generally given to rum or foreign spirits, though brandy is called Pa-Lan-Ti tsiu.   Green leaf Chu, (bamboo) "Inflammable green bean," and many such.

[2] The goddess of the moon, the patroness of faithful lovers.

CHAPTER IX.

LIANG'S THOUGHTS WHILE WANDERING IN THE MOONLIGHT.

AFTER a short pause, he said he must return to the study apartment. In the garden he met with young Yao, who asked him for his company to purchase books and fans,[1] and they went out of the house together. They loitered so long that they scarcely noticed the approach of evening, and the sun had gone down behind the western hills, before Liang thought of returning to the study. "Last night" said he "I was following the peach blossoms,—my thoughts and meditations troubled me sorely.[2]

[1] A Chinese gentleman is never seen without a fan.
[2] Tore up my bowels.

The example of Tsui and Chang was present to me, but the chamber-maid refused to play the part of Hang.[1] From that hour, I had been captivated, and my slumbers were broken. I arose, and looked towards the bright moon. The moon had a watery look, and all was silence around. The wind bore the fragrance of a hundred flowers, and I fancied that a beautiful woman passed before me. How could I dream that, in this cold study, my heart should take fire? But she smiled, and smote me with a heavenly passion—boundless as the sea. Now I am whelmed in dejection, I have no companion but the moon. I did not believe that love could be the cause of anguish; but now my love-anguish is intolerable, and forces tears that I cannot restrain. With them I water the flowers. Heart wounded and deserted, I lean upon the balustrade, and the low steps which divide me from the chloranthus-flower are distant as is the horizon of heaven. I have no pleasure in the odour of the roses, and the song of the birds is discord." And he stood motionless

[1] The servant girl of Tsui, who enabled her mistress to communicate with her lover.

and purposeless among the flowers,[1] while the
piercing cold of midnight penetrated his garments. At last, he moved towards the peonies.
He heard the herald voice of a solitary goose,[2]
and determined to avail himself of this oppor-
tune accident to have a letter conveyed to his
beloved. Was it not possible that heaven had
instructed the bird while floating above, to witness,—to sympathise with,—to put an end to
his sufferings? He seized his lute,—walked
into the moonlight,—and sang the well-known
song, "The Phœnix sings unto his love."[3]

[1] Flowers form a part of almost every picture and every poem in
China. The favourite designation of the Empire is well known to
be Hwa Kwo,—the flowery kingdom.

[2] Geese serve in China the purposes of our carrier pigeons.

[3] There are many popular songs in China, and music is much
cultivated among the educated classes. Connected with it, are
many pretty traditions. One is, of a musical woodcutter, who was
surprised by a fisherman, while playing upon the harpsichord.
"Your soul is now wandering in the mountains," said the fisherman. He changed the tune, and the fisherman said, "your soul is
now wandering over the ocean." The fisherman gave him money
to pursue his musical studies, and promised to return. He returned,
but the wood-cutter was dead. He found only the harpsichord,
which he broke in pieces, saying: "There is no one worthy to touch
thee again."

One of the legends says that, an Imperial princess played so divinely on the flute, that the eagles descended from heaven to listen
to her. An ambitious musician aspired to her hand, avowing that
he could attract the celestial spirits. He was accepted,—they were
both transformed into genii, and transported together to heaven.

But fearing that the maiden was too far away to hear him, he flung himself down among the flowers, and sighed and groaned in wild despondency.

"O, had I known more of the world—had I been told of all the bitterness of love, I would not have left my home. I would not have abandoned the shade of the olive tree."[1] He felt the storming wind—blast after bitter blast—rustling his silk sleeves. "And shall I ever enjoy the blessedness, as I am smitten with the miseries of love? Shall I be for ever shedding these hopeless tears?   Shall I never, never reach the palace of the moon?"   After awhile, he wiped away his tears with his silken sleeve, and wended his way to the place of his studies.

[1] Not have attended to anything but study.

CHAPTER X.

WE have said quite enough about the sorrows of the student Liang, and ought to be following the lady beauties, so we will go back to the lady of the elegant boudoir. For many days she had lingered in the house of Lady Yao, but so peremptory a message had come to summon her home, that Lady Yao pleaded in vain for a farther lengthening of her visit. She bade her aunt farewell, and took her departure. Her parents lovingly welcomed her back, but she returned with slow and sad steps to her bed-chamber. Pi Yue took the keys and opened the ornamented door, while Yun Liang rushed forward

3

and pulled up the green gauze window blinds.
Li Chun brushed away the dust from the toilet.
Kin Lang perfumed the bed furniture from a
censer smoking with burnt frankincense, while
Yu Yen prepared the couch on which their fair
lady was to repose. Ku Ying came with fresh
water from the well. Yu Fa arranged the fragrant mountain peonies in their painted vases,
and Yu Ha eagerly desired her young mistress
to tell them all about the beauties she had seen
in the house of the Lady Yao.

"Well! it is a charming place!" she answered: "The trees and the flowers in the
garden never lose their fragrance; they smell
sweetly the whole year long. The fish-ponds
are like our own, but the peony thicket is more
shady and cool." Here, Pi Yue broke upon
the conversation. "But it was a troublesome
meeting with the youth that evening. Miss
Ma was there, so I did not tell you all about it.
But when I went to pick up the draughts on the
terrace, I observed that the student Liang had
not returned to his apartment, but was leaning
like a bewildered being on the stone balustrade.
He spoke to me,—he told me everything from

the beginning to the end. He made me believe that from the moment he saw you he had lost his heart,—that you had carried it away,—that his soul would dwell in your boudoir,—that he had no thoughts but about you, and when and how he could bring about an alliance? Could he not follow the example of Liu Lang[1] and Yun Lang, and make his way to the fairy land?[1] He rambled into all sorts of strange stories, but every word betrayed his inner agitation. It was truly ridiculous. What business had he to concern himself with another man's daughter? The world is full of affected lovers, who are always pouring out their nonsense into the ears of women, ever prattling of their woes and desperation; one worse than another. They swear they are sick at heart, and want to be cured by some lady physician. He wearied me to death with his prate,—would persist, in spite of me, with his sobbing and groaning. He held a flower in his hand,—he let it drop into the water,—the stream carried it away. What had I to do with his lamentations?"

[1] See notes to Chapter VI.

The young lady laughed out heartily. "There are, indeed, strange creatures in the world. There always were, and always will be youths like bees[1] or butterflies fluttering about in the breeze, and fancying all the flowers belong to them. Most of them are very wild in their notions, and cannot see anybody's daughter without desiring to possess her. But we girls must be cautious and prudent, and take care that evil communications do not penetrate into our apartments. I am here and he is there, and if he have any thoughts of love, cannot he find the way to reach me?[2] I have ordered a scarlet curtain to be placed between the

[1] There is a pretty legend, which says: "A youth, while sleeping was accosted by a maiden, who asked him to accompany her for protection against some menaced danger, telling him she was a princess in disguise, but he turned away from her. Soon after, he heard a hum, and he saw, entangled in the web of a spider, a bee, about to be devoured. He released the bee, placed it upon the inkstand, when, from the impression of its feet, it left the character, "Grateful," and flew away. He followed it with his eyes, and saw it enter a honey-comb which was suspended above; the disguised princess was a bee." It is easy to fancy that the character or sign meaning "Gratitude," could be made by the impress of a bee's feet.

[2] There is a Chinese proverb which says: "Thousands of miles of distance will not separate those who are predestinated to meet. But those who are not predestinated to meet, will not know one another though brought face to face." All Chinese romance is full of re-

flowers and the moon. The freed butterfly may fly over the northern wall.[1]

ference to the power of destiny, in overcoming every obstacle, and to the utter hopelessness of pursuing any object against the decrees of hostile fate. There is a saying, that nothing can prevent the interchanges of sympathy between lovers predestined to be united. " When we are unable to stretch our hands to one another, cannot our thoughts (by mutual understanding) mingle when the cock crows,—when the winds blow,—when the rain falls."

[1] An ancient legend speaks of a Chinese student who, being enamoured of a beautiful girl, was informed that his only hope depended on his obtaining the doctorial degree. He took an apartment outside the western wall of the habitation of his beloved, and having succeeded, she sent her invitation to him in these words :— " The butterfly may fly over the western wall," and the phrase has become the recognition of a permission to pay court to a lady.

CHAPTER XI.

OUR HERO SEEKS AND PURCHASES A CELL FOR
STUDY. ·

ENOUGH for the present of the discourses between the mistresses and their maidens. We
will again join our young, broken-hearted student.

"I hear that the charmer is departed,—I
know why,—it was her purpose to tear my
soul in twain. Yes! she has placed the curtain[1]
of separation between us. How can I approach
her? The pathway betwixt earth and heaven is
dark—is invisible. Why is my love unrequited?
Have I burnt unassorted sandal wood sticks at

---

[1] The sedan chairs, in which ladies are carried, have a red curtain
behind the glass door, which prevents their being seen.

the altar?[1] My sorrow is intolerable. I look by day, sadly on the jasper clouds, and, by night, I weep over my silver lamp. Under her malignant influences my frame is wasting away, and I have put aside the azure light and the yellow manuscripts.[2] I dream of her, but only to have my sleep disturbed,—all my purposes disordered. I rise—I dress myself—I wander here and there—my troubles always with me, and comfort nowhere to be found. But I must discover her abode." He questioned the servants and the slaves of Lady Yao, and obtained them all the same answer, "She lives in Tsui Hien Fung, in the palace of Mr. Fang."

And so he apparelled himself and sought out the abode of the illustrious gentleman. He found it, but no sign of woman was there. The place was extensive, but he discovered no living being to whom he could address himself. Was there nobody to whom he could entrust a letter, to be dropped into the ladies' apartments? Having looked about in vain on every side, he perceived a small, empty house near

[1] Neglected my religious duties. The proper selection of sticks to be burnt at the altar is an important act of worship.

[2] Abandoned my studies.

the palace, whose wall it touched. The red door was closed, and he directed his servant to make enquiries, who learnt that the house was for sale, that it was comfortable and spacious, had a pond and a garden, and that it communicated with the domicile of Yang. The information delighted Liang. " Now," thought he, " I shall be in the way to the palace of the moon; now shall I meet the nymph of the enchanted mountain; now shall I realize the dream of Kao Tang." [1]

He returned home, and said to his servants: ' Now, if anybody can help me to find access to the fragrant boudoir, I shall not think ten pieces of gold too much for a reward." He called in an architect and ordered him to prepare a commodious apartment for study,—a gardener was sent for to arrange the back garden, and he was specially directed to make a bank on the western side, and to fill it with the

[1] It was in the neighbourhood of Kao Tang that the vision of celestial beauty appeared to the Emperor Siang (see Note 2 to chapter vi.) She veiled herself in mystery, and refused to give any other name than that she was " the morning cloud and the evening rain." The legend is frequently referred to in Chinese romance; and, indeed, it is one of the popular stories which pass from mouth to mouth and from generation to generation.

most beautiful flowers, whose odours should per-
fume the evening air; a balcony was to be built,
overlooking that side of the parterre whence
the east wind was to bear away, towards the
boudoir, all the fragrance that cultivated nature
could furnish. On the north side he would
have a vernal bower filled with plants, the
rarest and the most admired. A stream was to
flow into the pond, which was to be properly
provided with gold and silver fish. The pond
for the lustrous spangles[1] was to be surrounded
with waving willows, and was to be amply
furnished with lotus flowers, both white and
red. There was to be a Bella Vista pavilion
on the eastern side, with adjacent elms to
shade from the dazzling of the many-coloured
clouds. Red bamboos and peach trees were to
moderate the fury of the winds. Descending
from the vermilion balustrade, there was to be
a richly-scented hall. At the entrance were to
be placed rare and beautiful plants and shrubs,
delicate rock-work, inlaid with flowers, and, to
the south, an arbour of almond trees. Day and
night the workmen were busy in erecting the

---

[1] Gold-fish.

3 *

balustrade; grotesquely shaped stones were gathered and heaped artistically together; little by little, all was arranged, so as to make a perfect picture. Pretty birds and rare animals were bought, and let loose in the garden. It was like fairy land. It was the palace of Kwang Han.[1]

[1] The palace of love and of chastity, presided over by the goddess of the moon. A common phrase in China to designate an unhallowed passion, is to say, "the red dirt is driven towards the palace of Kwang Han," of which the recondite meaning is, that though such a passion may put forward the pretexts of purity, there will be no protection for the woman who is betrayed, for the dirt will not be allowed to enter the palace.

CHAPTER XII.

LIANG took his departure from his aunt's, and had his luggage conveyed to his new abode, to which he invited his cousin Yao, whose opinion about the study arrangements he desired to learn. "Your uncle," he said, "the Major-General Yang, lives close by,—indeed, there is only a white wall between his house and my study. I want to send my card and ask for an audience. I hope you will accompany me to his library." "Most willingly," answered Yao, and they sent forward their cards of announcement into the Saloon. Yang, having seen the cards, desired that the two youths would have the goodness to enter,—which they did, making the becoming prostrations. After they had partaken of the fine tea[1] which the attendants brought in, the conversation began. Yao bowed again, and spoke: " Will you graciously

[1] Tea is produced in China in qualities as various as the wines of Europe, and at prices ranging from three pence to three guineas a pound. In teas of the highest value, every leaf is separately plucked and manipulated. Sometimes the leaves are impregnated with the fragrance of odoriferous flowers ; sometimes with the essence of herbs of medicinal virtues. When the Commissioner Yeh (by the way, *Yeh* means Leaf), was our prisoner at Hong Kong, the only courtesy he consented to receive at our hands, was to provide him with tobacco and tea of a special character, which he said he required for some bodily ailments, and which he enabled us to obtain for him in a particular quarter. Fine tea is never made in a tea-pot. A small quantity of the leaves is put into a cup, which is brought to the guests in an ornamented brass stand of an oblong shape, with curved or decorated handles at the two ends, and hot water is poured on the tea, but the cup is immediately covered with a saucer of the size of the top of the cup, so that none of the fragrance can escape, and it is sucked through the space left by slightly raising one side of the saucer, so that while the taste is gratified with the liquid, the smell inhales the perfumes which, as in the case of the finest wines, are quite as highly appreciated as is the flavour. Very few teas of the highest prices are seen, except as curiosities, in the marts of Europe. The teas purchased by the Russians for overland carriage by the caravans, cost on an average in China about three times the prices paid for the teas ordinarily exported to Great Britain and her colonies. Painted green tea is never used by the Chinese. The colouring is produced by a mixture of turmeric, Prussian blue, and gypsum, reduced to an impalpable powder, and sprinkled over the tea, which during the process, is kept in a state of humidity in hot open iron boilers.

listen, honoured uncle? My worthy brother Liang is my veritable cousin, and his father is the Imperial Chancellor in Wu Kiang. He is actively pursuing his studies, and, as he seeks peace and quiet, he has built himself, on the other side of your wall, an apartment for study, where I think of living with him,[1] and

Dr. Bridgman gives the native teas names of the various sorts of tea best known in the European markets :—

Pe Ko, or " white hair." Shang Hiang, or " highly fragrant." Wu I, or " Wu hills." Hung Mei, or " old man's eyebrows." Lin Tze Sin, and other names, such as translated, mean " Carnation Hair," " Red Plum Blossom," " Lotus Kernel," " Sparrow's Tongue," " Fir Leaf Pattern," " Dragon's pellet," " Dragon's Whiskers," " Small Plant" (Siao Chung, *i.e.*, Souchong), " Folded Plant" (Pou Chung or Powchong), " Working Tea" (Kung Fu, *i.e.*, Congo), " Autumn Dew," " Pearl Flower," (Chulan), " Careful Living" (Kan Pi, *i.e.*, Campoi), " Rains Before" (Yu tsien, Hyson) or " Plum Petals," " Flourish Spring," " Flourish Skin," " Tunkai (Twankay), Yunglo (Junglo), " Great Pearl," " Pearl Flower," " Skin Tea" and many more ; exhibiting not only the various qualities, but the fanciful designations appropriated to them.

The natives of the district call their mountains Bu-I (Bohea). Twankay is the name of a stream (in the province of Che Kiang,) on whose borders the tea grows. The Chulan derives its title from the fragrant flower with which it is scented. Oolong (Wu Lung, *i.e.*, Black Dragon), is become, of late years, a favourite tree in foreign markets.—See also, *Williams' Mid. King*, ii. Chap. xlv.

[1] Intimate communion and confidence between friends, is laid down as prominent among the social virtues, and their exercise is illustrated by much legendary lore. In Mr. Wade's admirable contribution to the study of colloquial Chinese, (Trübner, 1867) he translates one of the stories, exhibiting " friendship as it existed in the olden time." " Kwan Chung and Pao Shu were walking in the country. They saw an ingot of gold lying by the road-side. Each

we have desired to see you without delay, that we might present our respectful compliments." Upon this, Liang made a smiling, but most lowly obeisance, and said: "Your humble neighbour has built a house, upon which he implores you, condescendingly, to fling your favouring glance, and if you will honour my poor person with the benefit of your valued instructions, I shall be grateful for the favour to the very end of my days." The old man answered smilingly, "Your worthy father was a friend of mine at the Academy. In our early years we were like brothers, and went together to our first examinations. In the year, Lin Mao,[1] your father's name appeared in the list of "the pro-

wished the other to take possession of it for himself, but as they were unwilling to do this, they walked on until they met with a labouring man. They told him where he would find the ingot of gold, and advised him to appropriate it, that there might be no question between themselves. He hurried forward, but no ingot of gold could he discover. All that he saw was a snake with two heads. He was exasperated, and cut the snake in two with his hoe. He hurried towards the friends, and reproached them for deceiving him. " What ill-will did you bear towards me, when you told me that a two-headed snake was an ingot of gold? You have put my very life in peril." They were incredulous, and went back to the spot, where they saw, not a two-headed snake, but the ingot of gold, divided into two equal pieces. Each took his half, and they went their way together, leaving the labourer to his meditations."—*The Hundred Lessons,* p. 32.

[1] The 28th year of the Cycle of 60.

moted," but I failed,—my composition was rejected, so I flung all my books of prose and poetry into the river, took to riding, archery, and warlike exercises, and luckily obtained the highest rank in the military competition, and was rewarded with an appointment in the army.[2] I was advanced to the grade of Lieutenant-Colonel, and had the military commandership of the province of Che Kiang. Your most illustrious father was made Imperial Chancellor, and through his influence I was raised to be Major-General, in the South. This morning, I have the felicity of welcoming his worthy son, and I assure him that the friendship existing between our families shall not be inter-

---

[2] After failures in the literary examinations, it is customary for the Chinese to enter into the field of military competition, where distinction is obtained for feats of strength, skill in archery, and equestrian dexterity. Imperial rewards, such as jasper, jade or agate rings, which are worn on the thumb to help the management of the bow, foxes' tails, peacocks' feathers, jackets of silk, and similar marks of the favour of the Son of Heaven, are given to successful competitors, whose names are printed, and the lists are eagerly purchased. But though esteemed as an honourable secondary position. there is a great gulf between literary and military rank. The sage, or learned man, stands at the top of all social grades. Next to him follows the agriculturist, while the soldier belongs to the third class.

There is a Chinese axiom which says: " Let the brave soldier have the costly sword. Rouge and pearl powder belong to the pretty woman."

rupted or forgotten." He ordered a handsome repast to be prepared in the summer-house.[1] "I must have some private talk with you," he said. And they rose up, and went into the garden, and admired the rare plants and flowers, the graceful bamboos, the silken-leaved willows. The pond, the summer-house, the pavilion, the pagoda, the bridges, were all charming. In the summer-house,—Bella Vista,—they saw, hanging on the wall, verses, beautifully written on a flowery scroll,—it was the perfection of caligraphy. The pencil of a master had painted the willows overhanging the water; both students approached, and both read the inscription:—

> The mournful willows beside the pond,
>   Tell me who planted—tell me who?
> The flying bats flit beyond, beyond,
>   They trouble the waters in passing through.
> But the willows are there with their light blue leaves,
> And the men depart—who grieves? who grieves?[2]

The old gentleman laughed aloud as they read the verses. "Cannot you honour this trash with a laugh?" he said. "My daughter wrote

[1] If you want to find hospitable hosts abroad, receive hospitably, guests at home.—*Chinese Proverb.*

[2] In the city of Chang Ngan are many willow trees. Just outside the gate is the summer-house of the broken willow branches. When a friend is about to depart on a journey, he is accompanied thither, and a branch, torn from the willow, is presented to him, to make his travels auspicious.

them. Are they not errant nonsense? Bad rhymes—Bad rhymes,—but fortunately I have now in my poor garden a talented youth, who does me the honour of admiring my trees, and plants and flowers. Will he graciously leave behind him a memento from his elegant pencil? Then, indeed, will my poor belongings have an irresistible attraction." Liang smiled, and answered: "I am but a dolt. I have had no time to study poetry." The old man replied. "No apology. I know very well that no student can write more charmingly than you!"[1]

---

[1] The odes found in *Shi King*, one of the most ancient repertories of poetry, and whose collection is generally attributed to Confucius‧ have given a character to the productions of all succeeding versifiers. They consist of national songs,—Hymns used at the sacrifices,— many pretty pictures of nature, associated with moral maxims and out-pourings of passion. Some of the lines contain three words, but a greater number four. The monosyllabic character of the language, and consequent paucity of words, provide abundant rhythmical terminations. Here is a specimen, in which a maiden sings of her absent lover :—

> The reeds and rushes are green,
>   Snow-white the icy hoar,
> But who is the wanderer, seen
>   On the river's farther shore ?
> My eyes have followed him,
>   Where his weary footstep stray,
> And I dream in vision dim,
>   That I see him far away.

He called one of the waiting maids, and said to her, " The way thro' the garden round that side of the wall is too long. The ladies' boudoir is near at hand. Go there as fast as you can, and bring some sheets of flowered writing paper."

After pencil and ink had been brought, Liang took up the pencil, and these were his secret musings. " My mind is full of perplexity, and there are no means of communicating with the boudoir, but wait—a thought suggests itself—I will, in my poem, mourn our separation, —I will try to move the loving affections of that divine maiden. Perhaps, in her boudoir, she may learn the state of my heart,—how it longs that she should cross the milky way and seek the temple of the moon. He endeavoured to pair the verses of the young lady, and over the picture of the willow tree wrote:

> The willows wave to the winds of spring,
>   Their branches ruffle the pond below—
> But can a beautiful living thing,
>   Behind her crimson portal know—
> The sorrow and suffering night and day,
> Of one who is sighing far away?

The old gentleman greatly praised the poem,

taking to himself the credit of having suggested it, and he suspended it on the white wall, by the side of that of his daughter. Two sheets of flowery letter paper lay upon the table. Liang secretly took possession of them, and said he should go a round-about way homeward, as he wished to enjoy the scenery. But the old veteran insisted that he should first take a collation in the summer-house. So they went all together to the Bella Vista, till the sun's disc told them the evening was come. Truth to tell, the students got drunk, and were led staggeringly out at the great door. The two students separated, after mutual salutations.   Yao, to his home,—Liang, to his study.

CHAPTER XIII.

WHAT LIANG THOUGHT ABOUT THE LADY IN HIS STUDY-MUSINGS.

THE first thing Liang did on entering his chamber was to open the window and gaze upon the bright moon. The goddess was in full glory. "Here am I alone, weary with the love of that rosy-cheeked maiden. Six months have passed since I was parted from her. Her boudoir near? No! It is as far from me as heaven from earth. Her crimson door is barred, and she is invisible. My heart is torn in pieces with anxiety. My eyes are dim with overstraining. Could I have foreseen this—this intolerable misery—could I have believed that we were not predestined to one another,

would I ever have plucked the fruit of discord
—ever sought to taste anything so bitter?
Cannot I forget this girl? My thoughts are
always wandering,—my knees tremble under
me. I wrote some verses in the summer-house
to-day, and brought away two sheets of flowery
letter paper in my sleeve. Let me have a look
at them. How fragrantly the paper smells,—
and what pretty pictures are painted upon it;
what a gifted maiden she must be! She may
well be called 'the nymph of the precious
stone.'[1] I saw the nymph—that beautiful
being—but now a thick, black cloud divides
us!" He crumpled up the flowery sheets and
held them fast in his gripe. "To whom can I
confide my sorrow?" His tears burst forth.
"O, Yao Sien! for you shall I die,—die in this
garden of flowers." He had been so absorbed
in thought, that he was insensible to the cold
blast, till overcome with shivering, he flung
himself on his bed, and passed a night which
he thought would never come to an end. He
closed the window frame to shut out the light,
but the darkness brought no rest.

[1] The literal meaning of the name Yao Sien.

CHAPTER XIV.

THE LADIES AND THEIR CHAMBER-MAIDS READ THE VERSES.

WE have said enough, too much, perhaps, of Liang's woes. Yao Sien rose early in the morning to take her accustomed walk among the flowers. Both the ladies, with their chamber-maids, went into the Bella Vista summer house. "What is this?" they exclaimed, "more verses upon the wall." They ran forward, as fast as the golden lilies[1] would allow them, and read the

---

[1] Many are the traditions as to the origin of this designation. One says: "An Emperor of the Tung Dynasty, (who reigned about 1000 years ago) was so enamoured with the small feet of one of his concubines, that he spread flowers of leaf-gold wherever she was to tread, that the impress of her footsteps might be left. He carried the fancy farther, and had flowers engraved on the soles of her shoes. Hence the name of 'golden lilies.'"

verses out aloud.   Both Yun Liang and Pi Yue
cried out, "Who can have been here,—who
wrote the verses,—who hung them upon the
wall? Do the young ladies know anything
about them?   The old gentleman cannot write
like this; and see, Miss! they are written upon
your own letter paper!" Yao Sien smiled, and
said to Yun Liang: "I will tell you what the
chamber-girl told me.   A new student's apartment has been built hereabouts, and yesterday
the student came to pay his respects to papa,
and said he was my brother's cousin.   Papa
asked him to take a meal in the back garden.
I dare say Papa requested him to draw a picture.[1]   So it was that the girl came to me for
writing paper.   See! there is his name, Liang,
written at the side. I should not wonder if I had
been in his thoughts when he wrote the verses.
Do not you observe that the lines about the
willows are echoes of mine? I dare say he
means that I, in my boudoir, do not care about
his sufferings. I think his love must have
made him a little crazy.   Is he not cunning to

---

[1] In China, albums are common. Verses are written,—pictures
are drawn, and interchanged as memorials of friendship.

have located himself so near our door?" Pi Yue burst out, "Well, Miss! I should not wonder if you were predestined to one another. Certain it is, that these are very pretty verses. May not a clever lad and a pretty maid"—here Miss Yao Sien stopped her, but did not frown. "What do you know about such matters? You should take care of the proprieties[1] within the boudoir! Nobody must look upon the nymph of the moon.[2] I dare say he does not know all that the sages have said about forbidden pleasures, and what has happened to those who have overstepped the prohibited boun-

---

[1] Womanly proprieties—another name for virtues—are laid down in an authoritative book, written by a lady in the first century of our era, whose name was Hwai Pan. "The excellences of women do not consist altogether in the possession of extraordinary abilities or superior acquirements, but in being becomingly grave and inviolably chaste. Woman must observe all the requirements of virtuous widowhood. She must be neat in her person and in all her surroundings. She must be unassuming and decorous, whether she sits or moves."

[2] Upon the maiden, whose chastity is in the guardianship of the nymph of the moon, so Shakespeare—

> "The chariest maid is prodigal enough,
> If she unveil her beauty to the moon."
>
> *Hamlet*, Act III.

To the "chaste moon" everything is to be confided by a maiden in China.

daries.   But we are maidens, and we must not
prattle, nor think about these things.   We
must not allow the driving clouds that cover
the moon to disturb us, but look out upon the
bright hills and the clear streams."   And so
they went back to their apartments, accompanied by their waiting-maids.   But there is
an old proverb which says: "There are ears
on the other side of the wall."[1]

[1] Another proverb says :—" Deafness is a virtue, especially in the
neighbourhood of a woman's apartments."

CHAPTER XV.

MAJOR-GENERAL YANG RETURNS THE VISIT.

WE will wait a little before we relate what happened, when the gifted girl returned to her boudoir.

Liang rose early,—looked out of the window, and held a colloquy with himself as to whether, according to the laws of courtesy,[1] he

[1] There is a supreme board at Peking, called the Li Pu, to which all questions of ceremony and courtesy are referred, whose decrees are published in the Imperial Gazette, for the advancement of the national education. They settle all questions of precedence, and regulate all ritual observances—all forms of official correspondence—all gradations of rank and title—all modes of dress and fashions, and the position of candidates in competitive examinations. One department has charge of the religious field—the modes of worship—the government of the temples, and all matters belonging to the national cultus. The book of rites, a voluminous production, is the officially recognised code. Confucius laid down as a maximum, " Cere-

might expect a return visit from the Major-General. Having determined that it was proper such visit should be made, and that he ought, in consequence, to prepare for him a becoming reception, he ordered an elegant collation to be got ready,—invited young Lao to be present, —directed the garden walks to be cleaned, and the flower-beds to be put in proper trim.

He was not mistaken in his calculations. Towards mid-day, the announcing cards were brought, and the two students went to the door to welcome their guest, and to conduct him to the hall of reception. Tea having been served, Liang requested he would honour the garden with his presence. The summer-house[1]

monials belong to everything." To be unacquainted with the " laws of courtesy"—to be ignorant of the exact sort of attentions required on a particular occasion, would be an opprobrium to a man pretending to good breeding. The *Siao Hioh*—book of primary lessons—gives instructions as to the usages between hosts and guests—the doors by which the guests are to enter—how they are to be received—where they are to sit—the number of bows—the foot that is to be put foremost—the postures to be observed—the manner in which the courtesies of the host are to accommodate themselves to the ranks of the guests. I have sometimes seen terrible scuffles between the servants of persons of distinction, each contending for the precedence of their masters, or for the right to claim certain attentions which other servants refuse to proffer.

[1] Literally, perfumed evening hall.

was ornamented with shrubs and flowers, and they filled the place with fragrance, while the guests partook of the dainties of the table.

Conversation was lively, compliments flowed, and mutual esteem and confidence were strengthened. At last, the old gentleman said, —smiling when he said it,—" Worthy nephew of mine! Are you betrothed? When will you conduct a beautiful woman into the golden temple?"[1] " How can I think of betrothing, who have not tasted of fame or glory?"[2] The

[1] When the Emperor Wu Ti was young, one of the princesses, embracing him, said: "Won't you wed?" "Willingly," he answered. She pointed to her daughter, A Kiao. "Does she please you?" "If she will wed me, she shall dwell in a golden temple!" But A Kiao's history was a melancholy one. Her husband got tired of her, and confined her in the palace of Chang Mun. From thence, she bribed the poet, Sze Ma, with a thousand pieces of gold, to write various odes, still celebrated in the poetical annals of China, which she sent to the Emperor, pathetically painting her love for him, and pouring out lamentations over her solitude. They touched him for a time, and brought about a reconciliation, but as her beauty had fled, his fidelity was not of long duration.

[2] Ordinary conversation, in China, is imbued with the many well-known proverbs, which point to literary reputation, as the ladder which must be mounted in order to obtain official promotion. Many of these proverbs have a poetical character,—for example :—

" When pursuing your studies, you must not fall asleep in the garden of the butterflies, for flies and mosquitos are there, (to distract you), and you will not be able to look through the perspective which leads to honourable office."

" He, who has succeeded in obtaining literary honours, is as gold ten times purified, and more brilliant than the brightest gem."

General felt, however, that he was on delicate ground, and that it was not quite the occasion for giving utterance to his secret wishes, but he ventured to say: " Mr. Liang! my garden is on the other side of the wall. Come to me like a son or a nephew. Let my house be your house. Why should not our two gardens be in common? Make you a door through the wall. I shall not object. Let it be at the end of the narrow path, and, whenever it suits you, come through into my garden. We can, if need be, cause the door to be locked. But out of the two gardens we may make an earthly paradise." [1] Liang could not express his delight, but he feared that reconsideration might come, and that, in a more quiet moment, old Yang might alter his purpose; so he determined to lose not a moment, —sent immediately for a mason,—told him to abandon all the works which had been commenced in the southern hall, in order that the communication might speedily be made between the two gardens, and joyfully exclaimed: " Now, indeed, will the breezes of spring play among the peach blossoms! "

---

[1] One of the Chinese commentators remarks, " This was bringing serpent into the house, to devour the chickens."

CHAPTER XVI.

TALK ABOUT A SON-IN-LAW.

THE old veteran, who had greatly enjoyed the
· collation, and had taken not a drop too little
of the eloquence-inspiring wine, found his
way safely home, and began to convey to his
wife the overflowings of his uppermost thought.
" That's a clever fellow,—that young student
Liang,—a wonderfully clever fellow. I am
sure he will make his way to the presence
of the Supremely August.[1] But how shall we

[1] Various are the adulatory names of the Emperor,—the usual
title is *Tien Tze,*—"Son of heaven," or, *Hwang Ti*, the "august
ruler." Another title is, *Wan sui, wan wan sui,*—"Ten thousand
times ten thousand, ten thousand years," in other words, " The
everlasting." He is sometimes called *Tien Hwang,* " Divinely
august," or, *Tien Ti,* "celestial ruler," and there are other designa-

tions, associating his name with the attributes of deity. "The golden mouth" is employed, when his Majesty is supposed to speak. His countenance is called "the dragon's face;" "the vermilion pencil" is that with which he writes. But he speaks of himself in terms of extreme humility, and, though sometimes using " *Chen*" " We," or "ourself," the titles he ordinarily employs, are " *Kwa Jin*,"— "The solitary man," or " *Kwa Kiun*,"—"The lonely prince." The sovereignty over all the earth, claimed by the Emperor of China has received an awful shock by the visitations of western nations.

The position of the Emperor of China is very extraordinary. Invested with an authority, believed by the multitudes to be supernatural and divine, honoured with titles which can only be properly applied to the Godhead,—the checks which have been placed upon his despotism by the sanction of tradition, and even by official machinery, are as curious as they are instructive. In the Siao Hioh the universally accredited manual for the instruction of youth, obedience to the Prince is made contingent on his observing "the rule of reason."

Of Yao, whose reign began, B. C. 2356, it is recorded in the Historical Classics :—

"The Emperor, having ruled over the empire fifty years, rambled through the highways and byeways, when the boys sang a ballad, saying, "He, who has established the multitude of us people is none other than your highness ; we know and understand nothing but to obey the Emperor's laws." There were some old men, however, who smote the clods, and sang along the roads, saying, 'At sunrise we engage in labour, and at sunset we rest ; we dig our own wells, and drink ; we plough our own fields, and eat ; what does the Emperor's strength avail us ?' He then made the inspection of the Hwa mountain, when the warden of Hwa felicitated him, saying, 'May the august individual become rich, enjoy longevity, and have many sons.' The Emperor said, 'I had rather be excused : he who has many sons has many tears ; he who is rich has a load of anxieties, and longevity is frequently attended with much disgrace.' The warden said, ' When heaven produces people, it always affords them employment ; thus, should you have ever so many sons, if you will give them something to do, what need you fear ? Be rich, and di-

vide your wealth among others ; then, what anxiety will you have ?
Should the empire possess the right way, you may prosper with the
rest ; but should the world be wicked, you have only to cultivate
virtue, and retire into obscurity ; then, when life is done, disgusted
with mankind, you depart and join the genii ; and whilst you ascend
yonder bright cloud, and mount to the regions of the Supreme,
where will be the disgrace ? ' "—*Medhurst's Translation of the Shoo
King*, p. 331.

And, again, of the Emperor Shun, (B. C. 2254) :—

" The Emperor encouraged the expression of public opinion, and
sought for men of talent to aid him in his government ; he was
willing to receive reproofs in order to be made acquainted with his
mistakes, and set up a board, on which people might state their com-
plaints, that all his subjects might expose his faults ; while he appointed a drum for those who dared to animadvert on his measures,
so that everyone had an opportunity of expressing his opinion."

" Shun married two of the daughters of Yao, who resigned to him
the Imperial throne. A curious account is given of the manner in
which his father-in-law " tested his talents and virtue" before the
abdication in his favour. He was called upon to explain and give
evidence of his obedience to the five fundamental laws of the Empire.
He was required to solve a hundred arithmetical questions, which he
did without a mistake. He was ordered to receive guests at the four
portals of the palace, and he observed all the becoming ceremonials
and preserved perfect harmony. He was sent, in the midst of violent
storms, thunders and rain, on a tour of agricultural inspection, at
the foot of the mountains, and he discharged his duty most satis-
factorily."—*p.* 332.

A festival is held on the fifth day of the fifth moon, called the
Dragon festival, in which, processions of boats, with great display and
noisy music, are seen on all the rivers of China. It is in honour of
a martyr minister, who, having vainly exhorted one of the Emperors
to discontinue his evil courses, and, instead of listening to his concubines, to attend to the councils of his ministers,—presented a
written protest to his master, saying, he would not live to see the
ruin of the Empire, and that he had determined to drown himself,
on a certain day,—which he did ; his body not having been discovered,
the anniversary of the day is still kept, in the expectation that the

induce him to send the crimson card[1] to our house?"

"It would really be a good match," said the lady, "his father is a Minister of State, and a

corpse will be found,—when honourable burial will be given to it, and the spirit of the dead find repose.

[1] Crimson cards, in China, play a very important part in matrimonial arrangements. I have known more than a dozen employed in the progress of the negociations, by which every stage and step is recorded, up to the final consummation. They are mostly about a foot in breadth, and some are many feet in length, with various adornings. In the Chi Hwa (Poetical Apophthegms) is the following legend.—"In the time of the Tung dynasty, (A. D. 874-88), Yu Yu found, floating in the moat of the Imperial palace, a red leaf of a tree, on which the following verse had been written with a stile.

> Why do the waters so swiftly flow?
> I live in my chamber and dwell on my woe,
> On the wandering waters the red-leaf I throw,
> Will no generous mortal pity my woe?

Upon which, Yu Yu took up another leaf, and wrote—

> Your message of grief I have read, pretty one!
> To whom shall I answer?—Just say—and tis done!

At the ebb of the waters, a Court lady, named Han, saw the swimming leaf, and picked it up. Soon after, Yu Yu became the governor of the children of Lord Han, who was the Imperial minister. At the time when the Emperor dismissed three thousand officials, Yu Yu was taken into favour, and Han gave him his relative, Lady Han, for a wife. During the progress of the espousals, each produced a casket, with a red leaf. "How strange!" everybody exclaimed. "Here is predestination!" "Was it not," said Han, "a very pretty poem that floated to me on the water, after my ten years of solitary musings? It is as it should be,—the phœnix has found a wife. The red leaf is a benevolent match-maker!"

4 *

distinguished man. It is a capital chance,—cannot you drop a word quietly, and arrange for a visit to him from the go-between.[1] We can find many ways to help the matter forward, which will fulfil the wish of our hearts." The old gentleman nodded to his wife: " He has got a handsome garden with hundreds of rare flowers. Do you know he is opening a passage into ours? If the days lengthen, depend upon it, I shall find a reasonable excuse for visiting him. I already love him as if he were my own son; to talk with him will be the delight of my old age."

[1] The Mei Jin or match-makers. All marriages between persons of rank, in China, are arranged by professionals, who settle the conditions, so that the parents of the bridegroom and bride may have no personal controversy. The correspondence is often carried on over a considerable period, and it frequently happens that the wife is never seen by the husband, until, after the final arrangements, she is conveyed to her future domicile, in a splendid, closed sedan chair, followed by her dowry, and accompanied by a long procession of friends, with various emblems, flags, and music.

CHAPTER XVII

OUR HERO MEETS WITH THE CHAMBER-MAID AND CONFESSES TO HER HIS LOVE.

LET us return to our boudoir. Yun Liang rose up early, and in obedience to the orders of her mistress, went to the garden to gather chloranthus flowers. The morning mists covered and concealed the trees, but she heard the little birds singing on the branches, as if pouring out their matin songs to heaven. She passed along the eastern hedge, and entered upon a winding path. She saw what she had never before observed, a double red door in the wall. Curiosity impelled her steps. On the other side of the door entrance was an alley of shady willows. "I have heard something," she said, "about this door, and that there is a pretty garden beyond it." Her golden lilies moved more quickly, and she determined to draw nearer and to peep in. Beautiful flowers were there in such abundance that they almost stopped the way. The clear water of the pond was covered with lotus leaves, and surrounded by willow trees, whose branches were dancing in the wind. She saw a stranger sitting in the shade of one of the weeping willows. His looks were melancholy; his eyes were closed. When he raised his head, he seemed startled with the appearance of a lady, but he observed that her "hair-clouds"[1] were not in order.[2]

She was young, pretty, and he advanced towards her and presented a chloranthus flower. He remembered that he had seen her before. It was she who had been playing at draughts with her mistresses, amidst the shadows of the trees in the garden. Though he then traced her somewhat indistinctly in the light of the moon, he

---

[1] *Yun Pin.* The Chinese word for the chignons of the ladies.

[2] She had risen too early to attend to her toilette, and had walked forth with her hair uncombed and her dress neglected.

was persuaded it was the very lady he now saw in the full brightness of the day, and her presence sorely agitated him. "True, it is, that Yao Sien is the real cause of my misery, yet the sight of this girl makes me almost crazy,—but why does she hurry away? I hear her silken garments rustled by the western wind." He ran after her, exclaiming, "Stay, stay! Why should you be alarmed? Why should you avoid me? It was I who saw the lady playing at draughts. It is I who am languishing for the nymph of the moon. Take pity upon me. My flesh and bones are decaying. I cannot eat nor drink by day, nor find sleep at night. Tell all this, I beseech you, tell it to the lady of the boudoir. Help me, or I shall perish. What is the moonlight,—what are the flowers to me, whom love has blinded? I came here to seek consolation. Let me not faint and die in this garden!" Yun Liang looked upon him with a smile, and answered him with a sweet voice: "Who would dare to utter the unbecoming word in the boudoir? My mistress is an angel of the Jasper lake.[1] She has no un-

[1] Yao Chi, a lake in fairy land, in which the celestials bathe.

maidenly thoughts,—no longing for prohibited things. If you will listen to my council, you will not talk wantonly. Depend upon it, no indiscreet message will ever be allowed to pass the painted screen." [1]

Liang was sadly perplexed by her words. Some pearly tears dropped down his cheeks, but

[1] A screen or curtain inside the door of the lady's apartment, which keeps out the wind, and prevents the intrusion of strangers. The domestic relations between the sexes, in the highest social grade of China, are little known to foreigners, and the cases are very rare in which English ladies have been admitted to personal intercourse with ladies in the superior ranks of the Mandarin families. Some of the missionaries and their wives have found access to the middle class circle, and we know of a few instances, where our countrywomen have been received by the families of Chinese dignitaries. The Chinese, though they avoid naming ladies in conversation, have not the same unwillingness to talk about their inner domestic life, which is exhibited by all the Mahomedan and Braminical peoples. There is no absolute separation between the sexes in Chinese families, but the education of boys and girls is so very dissimilar, that their minds are trained to models wholly unlike. Commissioner Yeh,—the viceroy over thirty millions of people,—being asked, what were the subjects of conversation in the families of the higher orders, he answered, by a maxim of Confucius, "Waste not words!" Being farther pressed, he said: "The principal business of women is to learn the various arts of embroidery," but when it was remarked that they could not be embroidering from morning to night, he replied: "They must attend to the cookery of the family." It was then retorted: "But, surely, ladies of high rank cannot be expected to attend to the details of the kitchen. You, a Viceroy, would not allow your wife to prepare your meals!" "Yes, she must, and, as a mother, ought to do so, as a matter of course. Many great families have no cooks. The women understand the thing,—and there's an end of it!"

he answered: "Let me tell you that my love has cost me the loss of a half year of my life. Why is that love unnoticed, as if it were written upon water?" Then he sighed heavily —cried out, "O heaven!"[1] wiped away his tears with his silken sleeve,—bent his head,—and silently descended the balustrade.

Yun Liang was by nature tender hearted, and thought that Liang's love was sincere enough to deserve her co-operation. So she replied: "Do not sigh so, Mr. Liang. There are multitudes of rosy-cheeked ladies in the world. Why are you so obstinately bent upon Yao Sien?" A sigh, still heavier, came from the student. "Shall I tell you all? It was the beauty of your mistress,—it was the smile of your mistress that fascinated me. How could I forget that full moon, those blooming flowers?

---

[1] Appeals to Tien Ti—heaven and earth—are constantly made by the Chinese: and even in their communications with foreigners, when they want to give an impression of their veracity, they will point with their finger upwards,—then downwards,—and then place their hand on their heart. There is a famous aphorism which says, that the fundamental principle of all things must be looked for in "heaven, earth, and man." And the same idea is represented in many forms:—"Heaven above—earth below—man between." The principle is symbolised by an equilateral triangle.

What pains have I taken, what misery I have gone through, in order to approach her! For this I have exhausted every resource,—for this I have sharpened my vision. To meet her is the delight of my three lives.[1] I wanted to pour out my heart to you, that you might convey my words to your divine mistress. I little thought that, when I had the good fortune to meet you, that you would utter to me such cold and ungracious words. And so my life-dreams are to be disappointed. The nuptial tie is not to be linked.[2] I am never to see her

---

[1] A common expression, meaning "the past, the present, and the future."

[2] The linking together of bridegroom and bride with a scarlet, silken thread, as part of the marriage ceremony, is traceable to a tradition, that the Lao Yue, old lady of the moon, dropped a book, which was found to contain some threads of scarlet silk. She was asked what was her intention, and answered that, the threads were to bind the feet of the affianced together. One of the Chinese names for matrimony is "The old lady of the moon." When a youth inquired of the goddess as to whom he was united, she answered: "to a girl of three years old, the daughter of a fruit seller, who is to be found at the northern gate of the city." The youth went,—found the child ugly and of mean birth : to escape the degradation, he hired an assassin to kill her, who struck her on the head, and left her for dead. Fourteen years passed, when the City magistrate arranged for a marriage with a girl of seventeen, whom he had adopted and treated as his daughter. When brought together, she was observed to wear an artificial flower, and on the bridegroom inquiring what it meant, she answered, "it was to hide

again. Go, go,—take her my writings,—tell her of one who is dying of a broken heart. Tell her I cannot pass the closed double door. Tell her that the forlorn one is gone to his death-bed beneath the jasper peach trees.[1]"

Yun Liang answered: "Why torment yourself so about a young girl, sighing and sobbing all the day long among the flowers,—wasting the spring of your life? I pity you,—but I will touch the pulse of my mistress' heart notwithstanding. Perchance the wind may move the clouds in the blue heavens.[2] But if, in the still night, and in the cold water, the fish will not take the bait,[3] then the handsome youth and the beautiful girl are not predestined to one another.[4] Pack up your thoughts—go home—

the marks of a wound she had received when a child." He thus recognised the power of the old lady of the moon,—and his destiny was accomplished. The artificial flower is worn at weddings as a memento of the event.

[1] See Chapter VI.

[2] The youth is the wind—the maiden the cloud—the heavens are the temple of love.

[3] The Chinese have a proverb—"The fish will not bite in the night when the water is cold."

[4] The references to *fate*, or predestination, are almost as frequent among the Chinese as among the Mohamedans. They do not, like the Arabs, attach an Inshallah (if Allah will), to everything which concerns the future; but they have a proverb constantly on their

do not waste any more time in flinging the peach blossoms upon the running stream." But her words, and the tone in which they were uttered, threw over him a beam of pleasure, and he broke out: "I thank you heartily, fair maiden, for your friendly wishes. And if you bring me a kind response from the boudoir, your goodness will be greater than that of heaven itself, and I shall never forget the blessed day—never—till my body is crumbled into powder. I cannot master my feelings,—do you come to their aid." She listened to his last words and hastily hurried home after saying "Farewell!" As she passed through the willow alley he called after her: "I forgot to ask your name and pre-

lips, "Jin shwo: joo tze joo tze: Tien shwo: wei jen, wei jen," of which the verbal rendering is, "Man says, So! so!—heaven says, No! no!" but the negation is singularly emphatic in the Chinese. It may be remembered that the Emperor Napoleon said the sublimest word he had ever heard was the *Não!* of the Portuguese minister, when he proposed his schemes for the invasion of the Peninsula. I believe, in almost every European language, the proverb "Man proposes and God disposes," is to be found. The Germans say, "Der Mensch denkts, Gott lenkts.—Man thinks, God governs." The Spaniards have the proverb in many shapes. One has all the Castilian grandiloquent sonorousness, "Los dichos en nos, los hechos en Dios." "The words are ours, the deeds are God's." The Dutch have a very trading-like, but nationally characteristic, form, "De Mensch wikt, maar God beschikt." "Man weighs (the commodity), God settles (the account)."

name, and how many beauties there are in the boudoir." She stopped an instant. " My name is Yun Liang, and there are eight of us, with our young mistress.   Your slave, with her companion, Pi Yue, have dwelt for ten years in the inner apartments of our mistress. None of us have ever left her.   And where could we find her equal? We live all like sisters together, and every day are in the garden, as gay and as happy as nymphs." [1]   Having said this, she passed through the garden, and he saw her shadow vibrating to and fro as she lifted the golden lilies. [2]

---

[1] Female slaves are so completely domiciled in China, that they are seldom sold by their owners, except in cases of great adversity and distress.   The legal authority is, however, absolute, as may be seen in an ancient proverb: "As the stocking cannot be freed while the boot covers it,—so cannot the slave be freed without the consent of the master."

[2] It is a compliment to a Chinese lady to say that she vibrates with the breeze.   The small feet makes her walk unsteady.   I have seen ladies take hold of a near object to prevent them from being blown over by the wind.

CHAPTER XVIII.

LOVE MAKES ITS WAY TO THE BOUDOIR.

WHEN Yun Liang returned to the toilette chamber, and had saluted her mistress, the *cicadæ* were singing on the flower-stalks.[1] She presented a chloranthus. flower to adorn the hair of the young lady. Yao Sien said immediately to her: "It was nearly dark when you left, and now the sun is shining on the balustrade. What made you stay so long in the garden?" Yun answered: "I went to the garden because you ordered me, and saw what I had never seen before,—a new door which opened into another garden. I was

[1] Shewing that the day was advanced, as the cicadæ never appear among the flowers till the morning dew is dried.

anxious, of course, to know what it meant,—so
I approached, but very timidly, and discovered
a student's apartment. At every step there
were fragrant flowers and singing birds. I went
forward, and under the shade of a willow tree,
I saw a melancholy youth, quite silent, but
most sorrowfully weeping. Immediately on
his perceiving me, he came forward and told
me a long story about his secret love. He said
he had seen a lady playing at draughts, and that
the sight had cost him six whole moons of
idleness and misery,—that his wretched life
was coming to an end,—that he could neither
eat nor drink,—he was, indeed, nearly crazed.
He said he had made a hundred attempts,—
employed a thousand devices to approach you,
—that he had spent a " thousand pieces of gold"[1]
to buy the garden, that he might be near you,
but he was still too far off, yet dreamed that
your heart and his might be one, and that you
might both live together for a hundred years.
I reproved him, and said you were as cold as

---

[1] In this, there is a recondite compliment, associating by a periphrase the garden with the fair lady,—one of the titles given to a
pretty girl being " A thousand gold pieces."

ice and pure as jade,[1] and could not allow his love dreams to disturb your rest. Hearing this, he broke out into loud lamentations, and rivers of round pearly tears watered the flowers. And he said: ' Will this beauty bring me to perdition? Shall the falling of my peach blossoms be recorded on the white wall?'[2]   The words were so impassioned, I could not bear to hear them. His heart was sorely troubled. I could not help pitying him. I remembered what a handsome youth he was when we first saw him in the lamp-light,—so gay,—so charming; but now he is reduced to a wretched skeleton; and I fear me he is doomed. Can it be of illicit love?"   These were heart rending words to Yao Sien, and she rose up and looked very miserable; she was silent,—seemed lost in thought,—but soon her lovely lips uttered these words: " I did believe there was some meaning in those lines, but never knew that his affection was deep as the ocean. Youth easily becomes demented. Is not his father a Minister at

---

[1] "Unspotted as the purest jade," is the ordinary designation of a chaste maiden.

[2] Must my epitaph be written ?

Court?   His talents and his bearing really resemble those of a sage of the ancient time.[1]
He is truly like a golden branch with jasper
leaves.   Is it not odd that such a man should
get entangled in the nets of love?   Well,—let
him look about for a 'go-between.'[2]   Perhaps
he may find some solace for his sorrow,—perhaps his moon will wax to the full."[3]   And
then, in a low, sweet voice, she said, " Yun
Liang ! we must not talk about this.   We
have been like sisters; we have been quite
alone.   It was you, who, by your dolorous
story, forced me to say what I ought never to
have said.   I have been very foolish.   Do not
expose me ; never let a word escape you,—not

---

[1] The *ne plus ultra* of a Chinese compliment.   The Book of Odes
says : " Have your ancestors—the sages of old—constantly on your
thoughts.   Talk constantly of their virtues, and learn to imitate
them."

[2] The employment of a match-maker is represented in one of the
Chinese classical works as the distinction between men and beasts.
" Men employ a go-between for the arrangement of marital affairs,
—which beasts do not."   No doubt, the axiom has been found very
useful to the marriage brokers.   It would be, however, a great breach
of decorum for a lady to be concerned in commissioning the match-
maker.

[3] A full moon represents perfect success—perfect happiness—a
completeness, which leaves nothing to be desired.

a single word."[1]   Something more might have
passed, but they were sent for to the presence
chamber.   Yao Sien rose, and, followed by her
maid, the golden lilies left the odoriferous
boudoir.

---

[1] Robert Thom, to whom I am indebted for many elucidatory
notes, and whose contributions, for the aid of English students of
Chinese, are most valuable, remarks, in his translation of " The lasting (literally, hundred years) resentment of Miss Keaow Lwan
Wong, on the extreme familiarity which exists between young ladies
and their female attendants."   Many of the Chinese waiting-maids
are very accomplished, and they often live on terms of great intimacy
with their mistresses.   Some are the children of respectable families
who have been compelled by want to sell their daughters as domestic
slaves,—others are bought by women who deal in feminine beauties,
—have them trained in the needful accomplishments, and sell them to
become hand-maidens to the highest bidder.

CHAPTER XIX.

ANOTHER MEETING WITH YUN LIANG.

THE conversation with Yun Liang had not been altogether satisfactory to the student. "She is light hearted,—she will be forgetful,—she will be laughing with her mistress in the fragrant boudoir, and for me, in my sleepless solitude,—why should she care for me? Why should she not be a cunning deceiver like the rest of womankind! It is in their nature to sport with our sufferings, and the prettier they are the more likely to do so. There was something deceitful in her eyes. The more I think the more my thoughts are shrouded in gloom. I put my elbows on my knees, and support my

5

aching head on my hands, and the more I ask for aid the less I find it. And this is all about a girl who is but a spring flower. And I pine and pine away. I only prayed that I might meet her. I met her, and the meeting has increased my misery and multiplied my tears. What is to be done?" He arranged his garments[1] and walked into the garden. He looked around, particularly towards the willow walk, but he saw no one. The cawing crows were taking their homeward flight, and the twilight of evening was growing darker. He passed into the outer garden and glanced at the flower beds. In mournful mood, he made his way to the balustrade, looked upon the red bamboos, which were waving in the wind, and on the little birds which were singing on the branches. But he heard the rustling of a silk garment in the bushes,— and, lo! with graceful steps, he saw Yun Liang, who had entered the garden. " Best of women !" he cried, for he was in a transport of joy, " You are come to confide to me the sweet secret, to bring the heavenly message from the

---

[1] The arrangement of garments, according to "the proprieties," is an important matter in Chinese education.

heavenly nymph." " Not so fast,—that is not so easy—not a word has she said,—how dare you to think so meanly of her? Do not you know the difference between common grass and beautiful flowers? No, Sir! the heart of my mistress is harder than stone or steel, and if you think that the goddess of the moon is to condescend to look down towards you, you must first mount above the mists and the clouds in order to approach nearer to her.[1] However, I did say a friendly word[2] for you after I left you yesterday, and entered the odoriferous boudoir; in fact, I told her that your heart was withering,—that you were very wretched,—and that she was the cause. I do think that I made an impression, and that she

---

[1] "You must succeed in your competitive examinations." Such are the ordinary counsels given to amorous and ambitious students. In the "Lasting Resentment" we find similar advice. "I would recommend you, Sir! not to revel in foolish dreams. Exert yourself,—apply to your books, and obtain entrance into the forest of pencils college." Thus explained by Thom :—

"The sound or symptom of levity ought not to enter the chaste precincts of the harem. Study hard,—try to become a Hanlin," (forest pencil) or member of the Imperial Academy, the highest literary grade in China.—p. 15.

[2] Literally, "I helped you with the knife of my tongue and the lance of my lips."

really began to think a little about you. She
has not opened to me her inmost heart, but
yet I do fancy there is for you a little bit of
secret love, but she will not own it. We may
see what is to be said and done bye-and-bye.
But as for you, Sir! you are impatient and
impetuous, and want to break down all becoming boundaries; and if you do not mind your
manners, you must look for another carrier-
goose to bear your messages, for I will have
nothing more to do with the matter!" .

Liang vehemently broke out: "Bear with
me—bear with me. Let me say only one
word. Love thoughts cannot be trampled out
of the heart. In my solitary study, a day
seems whole years long; but to-day has been
a day of blessedness. I feel like a poor mortal
who has been favoured with an angelic visit.
I did, indeed, trust that you would help me
over the azure bridge, and then it was that I
dared to raise my head among the flowers.
You have brought me news to-day which has
given me new life,—which has made me young
again. And now, dear girl! do not abandon
me. You have helped me half-way forward.

Pray help me still, for if you fail me, I shall fling my bruised and broken life down at your feet."

Yun Liang burst into loud laughter. " Well! and if you die at my feet, I shall witness the departure of a joyous and fortunate ghost. Love-thoughts live eternally in this changing world, though year after year the green spring takes its departure." Notwithstanding the laughing and the talking there was still darkness in the heavens. She took leave of the student, and the golden lilies conveyed her homeward. Liang would have charged her with ten thousand messages, but crowded them all into the words: " No delay,—my life is in your hands. Come back to the garden soon—soon." Yun Liang just bowed her head, —walked speedily away, and Liang retreated to the eastern garden.

CHAPTER XX.

THE LADIES AND THEIR CHAMBER-MAIDS STUDY THE MOON.

WE will now leave the youth among the flowers and pay a visit to Yao Sien, in her boudoir.

It was at the beginning of autumn, and the moonlight was magnificent. She ordered Yun Liang to roll up the ornamented curtain behind the door, and, followed by her maiden, she walked out upon the balustrade, to look upon the beautiful orb.[1] Its beams were brightly

[1] It is a Chinese fancy, that youths and maidens, when separated from one another, may see the face of their lover reflected in the full moon. This may excuse the perpetual and almost monotonous introductions of the silver orb in the scenes of romance. One of the common titles of the moon is "The jade stone mirror."

reflected on the water below, gentle breezes bore towards the ladies a delightful fragrance, and the shadows of the flowers were trembling on the wall.   And the young lady Yao remarked to Yun, in a very soft voice : " It seems to me that the four seasons linger in order to enjoy the sweetness of the atmosphere.   And we have passed through half the autumnal season.   I do not see a single cloud, and the moon is at its full. See how its beams dance upon the waters. Listen how the breezes are playing among the willows." Pi Yue, who was standing close to her mistress, took up the theme.   " But we are driven on- ward year after year.   The cold north wind will soon blow through the painted door. As we change our garments, so the world changes its face.   The flowers bloom,—the flowers fade, as summer and winter come.   The moon is bright, the moon is clouded by turns.   The returning springs bring old age to youth, and while men sleep, their hairs grow white.[1]   I recollect what passed in the beginning of the year.   More than six months have fled in the twinkling of an eye.   Some years ago I planted a row of

[1] A succession of proverbs.

weeping willows. They were small and weak, but not as high as my shoulder. Not long ago, I saw them tall and strong. I counted the years upon my fingers, and wondered that I had planted them so long ago, and now are they torn and stricken by the western wind,— their leaves are yellow and withered,—their freshness gone. And the life of man resembles a weeping willow. His middle life is like the beginning of autumn. Autumn departs,—the tree withers—the leaves fall—the countenance of man bears the marks of decay—but who shall renovate him? The green willow will be revisited by the reviving breath of spring; but who shall restore youth to the aged man?"

Yun Liang carried on the conversation: " So, in truth, it is, like the wind which scatters the clouds at the approach of evening; but why should we talk of these melancholy things, —that the trees lose their leaves, and that young men grow old; let us rather converse about the full moon, and about this lovely night. The world is full of variety. There are some who sit amusing themselves with the red-sided guitar. There are others, delighting themselves with idle revelries. There are hunting nymphs and nymphs running after ghosts, —who are groaning in helpless despair. Some are invoking the moon goddess to take pity on their woes. Some are travelling, thinking of their beloved and distant home, and in their sorrow would extinguish the very shadows of the moon. Others are dreaming of the absent, preparing warm garments for their return, but who knows whether those garments will ever be worn?[1] Then there are those whose thoughts

[1] This refers to a famous maxim of Confucius. "While your parents live, do not travel far away," on which there is a popular annotation, by a great authority, Ti Wen :—

"He who travels far away is apt to forget his parents, and, hence, is properly reprimanded by the sage. In truth, a long absence, can it be anything but a forgetfulness of father and mother ? Ought he not to remember that, in his infant helplessness, he was nurtured by their hand, and what would have been his fate had they abandoned him ? Could they have borne the sorrow of long separation, and how can he ? The thoughts of the wanderer will be wandering thoughts. And if absence be reprehensible,—long absence must be much more reprehensible. Can there be a greater privilege than to sit at the feet of our parents and be partakers of their joys ? How can they, who enjoy such a privilege, willingly abandon it ? If he quit his country, will he not ascend a mountain—whether barren or green—to get a look at the distant palace (home). What greater pleasure for parents than to see obedient children around them, enjoying, with them, their domestic happiness. How can they be obedient if they desert their home ? Think of the sorrow which memory will bring to parents, when they leave their door,—look to the end of their street,—and then to heaven,—but the son is far away.

cannot be reached,—perhaps they are rambling in their dreams to the terrace of the sun, and they awake to see the moon in the sky.[1] And these are truly worthy of compassion. Other wanderers there are, who delude themselves with the fancy, that after death, their emancipated spirits may fly towards the place of felicity. Some miseries may be removed, but love-thoughts are the worst of miseries, and make men dread to be left alone. I do not believe the full moon knows how many, and how grievous are the sorrows of mankind, or she

And what apprehensions fill the parental mind! The absent one is driven by the storm—he is blinded by the dust—the nights are bitterly cold—and he is left in loneliness—he travels over mountains—he meets with impediments,—and they are not on his homeward way; he speaks—his voice cannot be heard—his figure cannot be seen at the distance of a thousand *Li*. Is he to be embraced by his father? It cannot only be in his father's dreams,—the absent spirit is no better than a phantasm. A day to him is longer than three autumns, but, in his father's house, three autumns are no longer than a day. The budding of the willows,—the falling of the rain,—all are reminders of him who is not there; and, added to all that they know of his positive sufferings, a thousand fancied sufferings accompany him. Two hearts may be united,—but what if ten thousand *li* separate two bodies? What, if tall mountains and wide seas divide them? Years pass,—means of living are exhausted. Where is the recompense? Surely, the sage was right when he said: "While your parents live, do not travel far away.'"

[1] That they are still dwellers upon earth.

would not shine—as she does—everywhere so brightly.   But, after all, we should make the most of life,—enjoy it as well as we can, for it will soon depart; every spring carries away another year,—and a hundred springs would but bring life to an end, and when the end comes, Yen Wang[1] will claim his own.   Weal and

[1] Yen Wang, known also as Yen Kuen, in Sanscrit Jamarâdsha, is the judge who presides over the fifth of the Buddhist tribunals in the nether world, to whom is confided the inquiry whether a guilty soul may be allowed to return to earth in order to pass through another probation and to be purified from former sins.   He is painted with a dark countenance, sitting between two dogs, one black (*Zjama*), the other spotted (*Zabala*).

He keeps a book, in which every man's history is recorded from his birth to his death.   When he marks the page with a pencil, it is the death warrant, to which instant obedience is paid, and the mortal's history is closed.

On one occasion, when the book was getting old, Yen Wang tore out one of the leaves, and used it for the binding of the volume.   On that page was written the name of a poor man, Fang Tze.   Thus escaping the notice of the judge, it was supposed he would never die.

He was about eight hundred years old, and had married seventy-two wives, when his life suddenly came to an end.   On the death of his seventy-second wife, she was sent to the lower regions, where she was very curious to know how it was that her husband had lived so long.   It is said that there are no secrets for a newly-arrived woman.   An enquiry was instituted, and reached the ears of Yen Wang.   He ordered the book to be brought to him, discovered the missing leaf, made the fatal stroke, and poor Fang was gathered to his fathers.   *La Chine Ouverte*, p. 251; *Schlegel*, p. 95.

Yen is believed to possess great influence with *Shang Ti*, the supreme God.   He had summoned a virtuous man who had fur-

woe abide their time, but time abides for none."[1]

Yao Sien had listened attentively and thoughtfully to the conversations of the waiting-maids. Ten thousand seeds of love had been planted in her soul, and after she had been left alone, she arose and closed the shutters, to prevent the moon-shine from entering her chamber. She threw down the faded flowers that had adorned her hair,—removed all the enamelled ornaments which she had been wearing,—flung herself on her bed, and drew the curtains around her. Watch after watch[2] passed,— weary watches they were,—she was sleepless, —turning again and again upon her pillow.

nished three thousand six hundred coffins for the becoming interment of the poor, and when about to be conducted to judgment, the local deities, and those who had been the recipients of his bounties, so crowded the way, that the death-messenger could not enter the portal of his house. A petition was presented to the gods, that his life might be prolonged,—the prayer was granted to the extent of forty years.—Vide *Chinese Courtship*, p. 81.

[1] In the books of the sages there are many pretty, poetical allusions to the flight of time :—

"As the waves in a mighty river follow one another, so do the generations of men."—See " Chinese Moral Maxims," by Sir John Davis, *passim*.

[2] The Chinese day and night are divided into watches of two hours' duration.

She thought of the sad, but too truthful words of Yun Liang and Pi Yue. " I have lived sixteen springs,—dark hair and rosy lips will not long endure. Liang is languishing for my love. The chamber is chill and cold, and his spirit wanders away in his dreams. Among lovers would he not be a faithful lover? He is really a handsome fellow, talented, youthful, well-bred. Should I do wrong to encourage him? May we not be wedded happily together? " [1]

She felt colder and colder, though she pulled the coverlet more and more closely around her, —her restlessness increased,—and she passed the whole night in disquiet, even to the dawn of the day.

[1] Literally, " May not the top-knot be united." The hair of married women in China is arranged in a high top-knot.

CHAPTER XXI.

A MEETING IN THE GARDEN.

SHE rose, heaving a deep sigh. She leaned against the embroidered screen, her cheek resting upon her hand. Yun Liang heard her sigh, and at once thought it must be caused by the conversation of the last evening, which had left gloomy impressions upon her mind: so she said to her mistress: "My Lady! it is long since you took a walk in the garden. A great many new trees have been planted there. You must come and look at the flowers, they are so fresh and blooming. There is a new boat on the pond to gather the lotus-flowers. Let us go and see."

Yao Sien stood up and went into her chamber to comb and wash,—she placed no one of her golden ornaments in her hair, and apparelled herself only in a white silken garment which covered her crimson under dress. But simply clad as she was, she looked comelier than the goddess of the moon. "Come with me," she said to Yun Liang, and the golden lilies left their impress upon the fresh green moss.[1]

[1] The fashion of torturing the feet, so universal among the opulent classes in China, is said to have had its origin in the admiration caused by the beautiful small feet of one of the court ladies ; so beautiful, that the emperor caused the carpets to be covered with gold-leaf, in order that every one of her steps might leave the impression of its exquisite perfection. This excited the jealousy of the other ladies, and they endeavoured to torture their own feet and those of their female children into this envied exiguity. The admiration for these "golden lilies" extends to the lowest classes ; and to possess a small-footed wife is an object of general ambition. On one occasion, when I introduced some English ladies to Chinese women of rank, who saw our countrywomen for the first time, the Celestials shrank back, and we overheard the expressions, "What monstrous feet! What vulgar people!" and our hosts were requested to ascertain distinctly from me whether they were really respectable ladies, who could be properly and decorously received? One Chinese lady, after the first repugnance was overcome, and they had approached their foreign guests, whispered to her neighbours—"They are not such barbarians after all. They behave themselves very properly ;" and the answer was, "Yes, my dear! but you know they have lived for some time in Canton."

And so they entered the garden, and approached the lotus pond,—a mist was upon the water and they could not see the lotus boat. Yun Liang requested her mistress to come nearer to the eastern side: it was to bring her to the painted door, which she pushed open, and said, "My Lady! just let us have a peep into this new garden." "No! no!" answered Yao Sien. "I am afraid we may meet there the student Liang, and should he be there, how could we avoid him? No! I cannot go,—how can I look upon that sighing, sobbing man?" "He will not be there," she answered, "it is too early,—he is in the land of dreams. We will only look about for a moment. Why, you have already entered the garden." And Yao Sien followed the beckonings of her maid, and trod with trembling steps forward into the eastern garden.

It was really a charming place,—had everything to please the eye and to gratify all the senses. A varied landscape—fragrance from the flowers—songs from the birds—the clear water —the blue sky—the green shrubs. All fair, and serene and smiling; and who could suppose that it should be disturbed by the presence of an intruder? Yet so it was. Liang had passed a restless night and had left his sleepless bed. He was in the garden,—but concealed by the heavy fog. He heard the laugh and the voices of women, and ran towards the western corner, whence they proceeded. Yao Sien cried out, that men's footsteps were not far off. "Let us go—let us go," she said, without thinking that she was hurrying towards the very spot she wanted to avoid, but, perhaps, it was the thickness of the mists that prevented anybody seeing his way. A moment after, Liang lifted his head, and found himself in the presence of the unspeakably lovely,—the divine Yao Sien. A thousand agitations shook his frame, but he could not utter a single word. After a little time, he recovered himself, and said: "Fairest lady! to whom am I indebted for this felicity? Your divine apparition overwhelmed me. I have been paying my vows to the nymph of the moon, and implored her aid to save me from death. I petitioned for the meeting with which I am now blessed,—this auspicious meeting which assures me that, in our former lives, we were predestined to each other. Who can separate the snow, the moon, the wind, the flowers?[1] How short is youth, when youth is happy!" Yao Sien replied, as well as her shame and perplexity would allow her: "We have met under the plum trees and in the melon field.[2] You, Sir! are an honourable student, —your place is a cold study, and it is your business to be extracting sweets from the classics. I am a poor girl, hidden behind the screen, who have no better task than to ply my needle through the live-long day. My honoured parents manage all the household concerns, and a young girl is not allowed to speak of these.

[1] A Chinese aphorism; meaning that the snow flakes—the moon's rays—the currents of the wind—the odour of the flowers cannot be parted from one another—neither can the affections, which are reciprocal. As among the peasants of Spain, conversation is crowded with proverbs, as may be seen in all Sancho Panza's discourses; so in China, the aphorisms derived from the books of the sages and the traditions of the people, are employed on all occasions; and their appropriate use is considered evidence of good breeding and cultivation.

[2] This has reference to Chinese apophthegms.—"Stand not up under a plum tree;" "Leave not your shoes in a melon garden;" lest you should be accused of plucking the plums and stealing the melons. In other words—Be very cautious not to be found in suspicious places or under suspicious circumstances. This reproach is what Yao Sien applies to herself.

We must not carelessly break the bands of propriety. In the first place, we depend upon the will of our parents; in the second, on the will of heaven.[1] If I may counsel you, Sir! do not talk so carelessly and so wildly, but, with an upright heart, dedicate yourself to your studies and to the service of the supreme ruler."[1]

"Admirable woman!" he exclaimed, "how can I be ignorant of the laws of propriety! I have never violated them in thinking of you; with you I must be linked, or my green youth will be withered. But we must be obedient to our parents, notwithstanding all the prattle of the go-betweens. The world is full of vexations. Man is stupid,—woman is silent; this is, indeed, a matter for regret,—but listen to my vow,—I swear that my heart shall pass into your boudoir, if yours will stay in my study. We will, like the phœnixes,[2] be faithful to one another, and if you will not be wedded to me, I will be wedded to nobody."

Yao Sien smiled: "I believe everything is predestined in this world; the sages of old

---

[1] These are axioms strung together, and responses to the flowery phraseology of Liang.

[2] The birds Fung and Luan.

have told us that, if two persons are not pre-destined to one another, a meeting will avail but little. Meetings and partings are all arranged by heaven."[1]

She lifted up her head,—saw the sunbeams shining on the white camellias,[2]—was afraid that some of the servants would discover her in the garden,—so she took leave and departed, and the student walked back dejected to his apartments.

[1] The more frequently reference is made to the sages, and the more frequently appropriate quotations are introduced from their writings, the higher is the reputation acquired. A proverb says: "If you would measure the height of heaven, you must ascend the mountains; if you would judge of the depth of the earth, you must descend into the valleys; but if you desire to acquire all excellency, you must devote yourself to the study of the maxims of the ancient kings, (the sages of former times.)

[2] The fog was dispersed.

CHAPTER XXII.

LIANG TELLS HIS WOES TO THE FLOWERS.

LIANG was ill-satisfied with what he deemed the cold responses of Yao. "Little comfort have I got from this hard-hearted woman. I looked to her for healing, and she has inflicted another wound. She has added more wrinkles to my brows,—more sorrow to my bosom." And to the flowers he thus addressed himself:

> Flowers that so sweet and so abundant be,
> Pomegranates, in your scarlet livery,
> In your fair charms her fairer charms I see ;
>
> But her I see not ! so my heart o'erflows
> With weeping and with wailing for my woes ;
> And none will help me—none will interpose !
>
> Of her I dream—to her direct my cries,
> And tears of blood drop from my burning eyes,
> Red as the granate, or the evening skies.

Ye flowers as smooth as silk! thou lotus white,
Filling the air with odours exquisite,
Rising and falling on the waters light;

Yet, while I longing on the borders stand,
I cannot reach ye, though I stretch my hand,
Ye will not hear nor answer my command.

Where is the boat in my sore need to aid?
Where is the friend to guide me to the maid?

He threw himself back to find support from a willow tree,—looked around him wildly in the garden, his heart was fluttering like the reflection of the flowers on the face of the water, and thus he continued his out-pourings:

Your robes are lovely; but your loveliness
Than my fair maiden's garments charm me less;
More sweet than Olea fragrans is her dress.

I from the Kwang Han[1] Palace[2] brought a bough,[3]
But Chang Ngo's[2] help will not avail me now;
Alas! she has no smile upon her brow.

There the cloud-ladder[4] stands enwrapt in gloom;
There do the peach trees drop their roseate bloom,
And both remind me of my hopeless doom!

The double crimson door is closed—the screen—
There stands her beauty and my hopes between.
Of all the flowers, the Mow Tan[5] is the queen.

Who honours not the flowers,—the precious stone,
Who midst the fair loves not the fairest one.
Heaven's brightest star—worthy of earth's best throne.

1 Palace of the moon.   2 Place of literary distinction.   3 Goddess of the moon.
4 To mount the cloud-ladder, is to obtain the highest degrees in the competitive examinations.
5 Chinese peony.

All these are lovely, she is lovelier yet!
But my heart sinks—my dimnèd eyes are wet—
'Twas but repulse and coldness when we met,
And absence is dejection and regret.[1]

[1] These songs are generally extravagant, but are admired when, as in the present case, they are filled with classical allusions, and have fragments from ancient poetry intertwined. The association of flowers with literary distinctions is characteristic of Chinese poetry.

A well-known verse, to which Sir John Davis attributes an origin earlier than the Christian Era, but which Mr. W. H. Medhurst has traced to a poet, Su Fung Po, who lived in the 11th century, speaks of the successful graduates departing on a flying horse, through masses of blooming almond flowers extending for miles. It is to be remarked that, the first line of this verse is found inscribed on the porcelain bottles, whose discovery among the Pyramids has led to so much controversy as to the intercourse between China and Egypt. It is not impossible that Su introduced into his ode a quotation from an earlier poet. Sir H. Parkes states that, the stanza of five characters, in which these lines are written, was not known in China until the 2nd century of our era. Liang's verses are in lines of seven, and six characters.

CHAPTER XXIII.

SECRET CONFERENCES BETWEEN THE LADIES AND THE CHAMBER-MAIDS.

LET us again penetrate to the boudoir, and listen to the talk among the ladies. Yao was not satisfied with herself. She remembered the vehement words of Liang, when, in the shadow of the flowers, he had told her of his love, and she was troubled with painful perplexity. Had she not listened to his plaintive language? Had she not seen his showering tears? And these were her meditations:

"What hankerings have these young men after forbidden pleasures! and this youth is singularly impetuous. But why should I, young as I am, allow my heart to be troubled with such idle matters? When I saw his gestures, when he talked to me of his love, I could not but look and listen, and his emotions have entered the boudoir. I wish I had never seen —I wish I had never heard him,—for I am more and more ill at ease. I might have prevented my troubles from being piled up mountains high. People say that love-thoughts are of all thoughts the most difficult to disperse or to discard. Whose fault is it, that the tranquillity and solitude of his study have been troubled? yet why should I not abide with him till our hair grows white and our cheeks become pale with age? Truly, we both bemoan our separation, and now I begin to fear that the servant-maidens are beginning to guess that— I am very unhappy."

Yun Liang was indeed acquainted with the true state of matters, and thus, with much gentleness, she spake to her mistress: " My Lady! your flowery countenance is sad and silent. There is a mist upon your spring-time mountain,[1] whence I see a stream of tears flows secretly

---

[1] A fanciful expression for the forehead of a young lady.

down. Day and night follow one another apace, and even years speedily pass away. And when the spring time is gone, we grieve to think that it will never return. Open your heart,—let us talk about more pleasant things, and put aside all gloomy cares."

Yao answered: "Put yourself in my place. The autumnal cold has penetrated through my garments. Time is like flowing water,—and it has brought me much affliction."

Yun Liang, availing herself of the confidence placed in her by her mistress, thus replied: "Old age comes on so stealthily, that we grow grey even in our sleep. The sages have said, that it is easy to discover an invaluable treasure, but difficult to find a faithful love. The time that is departed will never return. You said that the cold autumn wind was penetrating your thin garments, and that the student, who was mourning over his loneliness in his dreary chamber, was the cause. Now, on the day when I met him, he said, and said only, this,—'that you once, twice, thrice had driven him to desperation,—that your heart was as hard as iron or stone,—and cared not if his were broken.'"

Yao Sien, then, as they were quite alone, confessed half and half,[1] to her maid, her hidden love: "We are like sisters,—I will hide nothing from you. Did you really believe that I was made of wood or clay, and valued faithful affection as little as worthless water? Who would not value a happy home? What celestial nymph is unwilling to be blest? But we must be guided by modesty and discretion, and avoid all reproach, and if the affair is spoken of, remember what bashfulness and propriety require. The student is a gay and indiscreet youth, and marriage is a very serious matter,—it is an eternal union. Perhaps he is only dreaming of transitory enjoyment. Man's love is fickle as the waves of the sea, and many there are in these days who trifle with women, only to deceive them, and who think the deceit is little better than a joke. And, after all, he may not be my predestined husband, or my parents may have other intentions. You spoke of so many useless, idle heart-engagements,—perhaps they will be handed over to another world as foolish love prattlings."[2]

[1] *i. e.*, wholly—reserving nothing.

[2] Proverb: "We shall be made responsible hereafter for our idle talk here."

Yun Liang answered, laughingly: "Best, dearest, and most charming lady! Now, I do not speak once, without having thrice thought of what I have to say. Liang is not a licentious adventurer. His speech is discreet,—his purposes firm as a rock. His father is one of the richest and most accomplished gentlemen at the Court, and his verses, odes, songs, and poems are known throughout the province of Kiang Nan. If he will only employ a proper negociator to arrange matters, sure I am that your father will put no difficulty in the way. A prettier face than yours is not to be found in the world. The plague is, one cannot always bring about a proper marriage arrangement. It is a very difficult business,—the old people are always looking to the go-betweens, in order to make a grand bargain. These fellows are paid for it, and they seek rank and riches, and care for nothing besides. They will find a fine match for any unpolished, stupid, lumping fool, if he have bushels of pearls, though he have nothing else to recommend him. They may bring a lady even to the throne of the Emperor, —but how many are there condemned to the cold palace,[1] and pining there in solitary misery. And still more melancholy for those who wander, like Chao Keun, beyond the border, no man knowing whither.[2] Not less so, was the doom of Yang Kui, who perished in her wretchedness on the Ma Wu mountain,[3] or Lady Yu, who fell down dead when she heard that her lover had destroyed himself by the side of the black

[1] The imperial concubines, after enjoying the favour of the Emperor from three to five years, are banished from his presence, and confined in a harem, called the Cold Palace.

[2] The Chinese annals relate, that during the reign of the Emperor Yuen, of the Han dynasty, B.C. 48—32, the khan of the Huns invaded China to obtain possession of the princess Chao Keun, one of the imperial concubines, whom the Tartar demanded in marriage. She was a poor peasant's daughter, whose singular beauty had led to her elevation. She had fascinated the khan, who had only seen her portrait. He invaded China, which was then in a feeble and disordered state, and he carried off his intended bride in triumph ; but when he reached the Black Dragon river, which divides Tartary from China, the unhappy princess pressed her beloved guitar to her bosom, and sprang into the stream, having first filled a glass of wine, which she drank in remembrance of her imperial master. The bereaved khan erected a magnificent monument to her memory on the banks of the river.

[3] Yang Kui was the concubine of Hiuen-Tzung (A.D. 713—56), She intrigued and eloped with the traitor, Ngan Lo Chan, who afterwards rebelled and brought the Emperor nearly to ruin. After his death, she fled to the Ma Wu Mountain, where she died of shame and vexation.

river.[1]   Or, Si Chi, who was drowned in the
five lakes.[2]

One there was, able to write a poem equal
to that, for which Siang Fu obtained a
thousand pieces of gold, but when she met the
prince in the harem, she had lost all her
beauty.[3]   Is it not better than to seek an early

---

[1] Yu was the mistress of Kang Yu, who contested the imperial
crown with Liu Pang in the second century before the Christian
era.   Liu Pang was founder of the Han dynasty.   Kang Yu, after
a battle, in which almost all his troops were slain, fled to the deepest
recesses of the mountains; but he was followed thither by Kwang
Ying, and, having no hope of escape, he cut his throat on the borders
of the river U.   His concubine died suddenly on hearing of his
untimely fate.

[3] Si Chi, or rather Si Sze, was a beautiful woman, who lived on
the western side of the Yo Ye stream, which runs at the foot of the
Chu Lo Mountain, hence her name—"the child of the west."   She
was a washerwoman, and gathered wood to burn.   The king of Yue,
who knew of the appreciation in which the king of Wu held feminine
charms, directed his minister, Chang, to kidnap Si Chi, and kept her
for three years, teaching her every accomplishment.   He then
directed his minister, Fan Li, to escort her to the court of Wu, and
to present her as a royal gift to the king.   He built for her a costly
palace, and, on his death, she determined to return home, accompanied by Fan Li, but lost her life by drowning in one of the five
lakes.

See Chap. XV.   It was Sze Ma Seang Yao, who, in consequence
of his reputation as a poet, was applied to by A Kiao, who, after
living five years with the Emperor, had been shut up in the Chang
Mun Palace, to write an "Ode from the Harem."   He sent him a
thousand pieces of gold, and he wrote the famous "Ode from the
Palace of Chang Mun," in which he touchingly recommended the lady

alliance! A talented youth and a charming girl do not always meet, and if you are so indifferent, and take no notice of him, he will return to his birth-place, and this precious pearl will fall into other hands, and you will never hear another word about him."

Yao Sien was about to reply to Yun Liang, when Yu Siao unexpectedly entered the boudoir, and Yao turned away, to look out upon the moonbeams that were shining on the water.

---

to the Emperor's favour; and painted so vividly the sufferings she endured, that she was recalled to the court; but her sorrows had destroyed her beauty, and she was not able to reinstate herself in the good graces of the Son of Heaven.

The ode, full of references to Chinese traditions, would not be intelligible to English readers. One of the verses says:

Si Chi, to wash her mourning clothes,
Leaned o'er the bank where the Hwan-stream flows,—
The moss and lichens upon the stones,
With jealous pity, heard her groans,—
Si Chi is gone—Alas! she is gone.
Why should the peach tree blossom on?

CHAPTER XXIV.

THEY SWEAR ETERNAL FIDELITY TO ONE ANOTHER.

LIANG sat musing on the beautiful form of his beloved.

"Light and darkness" said he, "regularly follow one another,—but the projects of men are constantly interrupted and disturbed. In the twinkling of an eye we have passed into the middle of the eighth month. The lovely one is departed, and has left no trace behind her. How can I bring my emotions into her presence? This evening is the festival of mid autumn.[1]

[1] The festival of mid autumn, on the 15th day of the 8th moon, is celebrated with great display in China.

What music, what rejoicings there will be! Flutes and viols will fill the air with their harmonies.   Everybody will be revelling in the bright moonshine.   But I am overwhelmed with sorrows, piled upon me mountains high. The golden cup will pour nothing into the mouth of a wretched one.   I have neglected— I have abandoned everything for her sake.[1] Goddess of the moon! why shine so brightly on others,—why so frowningly on me?"

He listened.   The drum at the tower of the city gate announced the second watch.   The light of his fading lamp was reflected on his pale face.   He lay down—wrapped his coverlet round him—shivered with cold—was restless—sleepless—so he rose, to take a solitary and melancholy walk.   He passed through the bamboo alley, but did not meet a living soul, nor did he even hear the rustling of the wind. On the lotus-pond, the moonbeams were trembling.   Suddenly, he heard the sounds of the jasper flutes, whose echoes resounded from hills and vales.   They brought momentary comfort,

---

[1] For a student to neglect his studies is deemed not only a folly but a crime, and the confession is the greatest self-reproach.

and two tear-drops fell upon his garments. He passed on, through the double door, into the farther garden. He was attracted by a distant object in the moonlight,—he hurried to conceal himself in the shade of the willow trees, and there he perceived a group of nymphs, and heard their silk garments rustling in the wind. Blessed sight! It was Yang's daughter,—it was Yao herself, wandering about in the moonshine with her maids.

One of them said: " The pictures of nature, how many and how beautiful they are! The moonlight is charming when it looks through the window, but how much more charming when it shines upon us out of doors, and we are walking in the soft breeze."

They never dreamed that any one was standing under the weeping willows, and looking upon that beautiful face,—but Liang sprang forward, and said: " O, auspicious night! Fair lady! Sympathise with me! Sweeten my whole life." But Pi Yue came towards him, and cried out: " Who has dared to enter this garden in the middle of the night? Depart! Is not my mistress here? You must have a

heaven-high courage to exhibit such effrontery !'
Hearing this, he said: " Forgive me,—forgive
me, fair lady!   Since I met her at the draught
table I have ventured to hope.   I have everywhere followed—everywhere sought her.   The
recollection of her has haunted the solitude of
my study and deprived me of my heart's repose.   The moon above is my witness.   Does
she not shine on flowers and trees and gardens?
And do not despise the poor student who, on a
night like this, gives utterance to his love."

She very sweetly replied: " Sir! Kindly
listen!   This garden is not the Woo Ling
ferry.[1]   It does not become girls to trouble
themselves about love.[2]   My business is to ply
my needle in my chamber.   Your business is
to pursue your studies in yours.   Go back,
therefore,—do not waste your time under the
willow.[3]   Do not be intruding on this side
the garden wall."

But Liang burst into tears, and called her
the lady of the stone and iron heart.   He re-

---

[1] By which lovers pass to the regions of blessedness.—See p. 27.
[2] Literally, " Distaffs and hair pins must not concern themselves
with the winds and the flowers."
[3] Paying attention to ladies.

proached her for having destroyed his health and peace of mind,—that she had interrupted his studies and marred his prospects in life. "I cannot tear up my deeply-rooted love. I call on the moon to see my tears. I wander despairingly about the garden,—irresolute and trembling,—not knowing whitherward to direct my steps. I am wasted to a dark bamboo stem in the forest, so that no one would recognise me. I cannot bear my wretchedness by day,—I am worn out by my restlessness at night. I cry out when I hear the beat of the drum,—the moon disappears and leaves me to my blank misery. Who can—I cannot, bear the pangs of love. I watch my wasting lamp while my heart is breaking. Fair maiden, if you doubt me, see that my garments are wet with tears. If you will not condescend to notice me,—I will die at your feet. I cannot hate you, though you have doomed me to death,—but you will compel me to believe that we hated one another in our former existence." [1]

[1] In this outburst of passion, the moon is the representative of the beloved one. The Chinese hold the doctrine that, the union of souls in a former state of being, precedes the corporal espousal in the present. If there were hatred in the earlier life, no love can

Yao Sien said: "J know you are unhappy," and Yun Liang observed that some tears had fallen upon her bosom,—so she sprang forward, and cried out: "Dearest Lady! his heart is sorely wounded,—do not pierce it with another murderous sword. A talented youth and a charming maiden do not always meet. Where did Pe Ya find a lover of his music?[1]   Follow

be permitted in this. The malignant gods sometimes encourage the passion of unrequited love in this world, as a punishment for the hatred which existed in the former. Such a state of things Liang represents as the extremity of woe.

[1] Pe Ya was a famed lute-player, who lived many centuries before the Christian era. He was a Mandarin of the kingdom of Tsin, and he was sent as an envoy to the king of Thsu. While crossing the river Han, a violent storm burst out, and the boat could make no farther progress. But the wind having abated, the moon appeared in the heavens. Pe Ya took up his lute, and began to play. A woodcutter was standing on the bank, and expressed his wonderment at the beauty of the music.

Pe Ya nodded to him, asked him to come on board the boat, and enquired whether he could play upon the lute. "Yes!" he answered. Pe Ya turned his thoughts to the high mountains, and the woodcutter said: "You are thinking about the high mountains." He played another tune, and was thinking of the running stream. The woodcutter remarked that, the music of his lute was like that of flowing water. Pe Ya praised his sagacity and asked his name. He answered: "Chung Tze Ki." They swore an oath of brotherhood, and Pe Ya promised to return the following year. He returned,—and, instead of Chung, he found a grey-headed man, who said he was Chung's father,—but that Chung was dead. Upon which, Pe Ya visited Chung's grave, over which he broke his lute in pieces, as no one was left in the world to appreciate his playing.

the councils of your servant, and swear the oath of fidelity which shall represent your inmost heart. Swear that your union shall never be broken,—that your purpose shall never be frustrated. Speak freely of your inclination. Put an end to' your own hesitation. —the world will know that you are irrevocably bound to him. You are not the first who have confessed their secret love. You cannot count the number of those whom pretty girls have fascinated."

Yao Sien did not answer a word. She looked upon the moon in her perplexity. Yun Liang,—cunning one that she was,—perceived what was passing in the mind of her mistress. She called on Pi Yue to come into the garden, and to make the incense table ready in the summer-house. As they went, Yao Sien blushed, and said to the student Liang: "I have seen sixteen springs, and have grown up in the boudoir. My door-screen has not allowed me to look upon vernal beauty. I have never wandered among the falling blossoms, nor gathered the opening flowers. I have only listened to the lessons of my mother,—she taught me embroidery. I have not dared to ramble even to the neighbouring village,—but your declarations have moved me, and I am willing to swear to you an everlasting faithfulness. But you must respect the bashfulness of a young girl. The oath shall rivet us to-day. Let it be irrevocable."

Liang replied: "My gratitude for your love and your virtue is as deep as the sea. The moon is my mistress. My heart will never change. My sufferings are rewarded."

He took two sheets of flowery writing paper from his sleeve.

"We will record our vows. Each shall have a copy,—it will perpetuate the rectitude of our hearts." There was a pencil on the lute table, and he wrote down the oath in the presence of the gods. He inscribed on the top of the sheet, the names and pre-names of both parties, then those of Yun Liang and two other servants as witnesses, and this was the record :—

"We met in the house of Lady Yao. I followed her footsteps, and found access to this garden. After a hundred difficulties, I was able to approach her. Heaven had predestined our meeting. We have sworn a mutual oath in the full moon,—and the full moon sheds its light upon our engagement. If the youth break his oath he shall perish with the sword. He shall be dashed into the fiery pool and never return to earth. If the maiden break the oath, she shall be flung into the river and not escape the axe, which shall divide her head from her body."

Having taken the oath, they knelt down, and selected their three sacrificial sticks,[1] that they might make their vows to the Deities. The first stick was the Ma Ya,[2]—which was an offering to the god of literature,[3]—praying that the

[1] In the initiations to the Secret Societies of China, three varieties of incense sticks are used, when the oaths are administered. By the first, the favour of heaven is asked for the faithful and the good. By the second, the thunderbolts of heaven are invoked on the false-hearted. By the third, the votaries swear to be loyal and united. —*Schlégel's Hung*, p. 124-5.

Three cups of wine are used for the libations. The first is presented to heaven,—the second poured out on the earth,—the third is placed on the altar of the temple.

[2] Ma Ya, Horse tooth,—(literally) these sticks are said to be made from the crushed bones of the sea horse.

[3] To the god of literature many temples are erected in China. He is generally represented with one foot upon the earth, and with a pencil in his right hand, directed toward the northern star. The constellation of the great bear is usually introduced, the pointers of which indicate the position of the central luminary.

votary might be admitted among the learned,
—that flowers might fall from his auspicious
pen,—that he might succeed in the spring
examinations,—that his fame might spread
through the world,—and that, clad in silken
garments,[1] he might return to his betrothed.
The second sacrificial stick was of yellow sandal wood.   To this, was attached the prayer,
that the tender-hearted youth and the rosy-
cheeked maid might have their requests granted,
—be united in one, and the fragrant fame of
their happiness be spread over the earth.   The
third sacrificial stick was made of aloe wood.
It was dedicated to the nymph of the moon,
imploring her to protect and patronise, and
make ever-during their first pure love.   They
swore that their vows were high as the mountains and deep as the seas,—that they would
never be unfaithful to one another,—but, that
as long as the earth should stand, and the

---

[1] One of the sages says : "He, who is clothed in silk, as the recompense of his literary distinctions, should exhibit himself in the
neighbourhood of his birth, for the honour of his family and ances-
try.   Not to do this, is to wrap up reputation in darkness.   He
should display his silken robes in the full daylight, in presence of his
fellow citizens, that they may see and wonder."

heavens should endure, they would follow in the virtuous footsteps of their forefathers.[1]

After they had thus knelt and thus sworn, they stood up, and after seating themselves among the flowers, Liang thus spoke:

♪"It was, dearest, as I remember, in the

[1] Veracity and truthfulness are certainly not among the characteristic virtues of the Chinese. They have a proverb: "Puh ta, puh chaou." "No blows, no truth," and they give effect to the theory by constantly employing torture, in their tribunals, when witnesses are supposed to prevaricate, or where their evidence does not accord with the foregone conclusions of the judge. I had, once, some men brought before me on account of the truth they had spoken. After the infliction of the blows, they made false statements, contradicting what they had before said. In the course of the proceedings, the magistrate, perhaps bribed in the interval, and desirous that the first averments should be confirmed, had torture again applied, and the men then re-asserted their early depositions. In our English tribunals, where Chinamen were called on to give evidence, these were the ways of administering oaths :—

The head of a cock was cut off, and the witness swore, by the blood of the bird, that the evidence he would give was the truth, the whole truth, and nothing but the truth; or, a plate was broken, and the witness called to bring down perdition on himself, and that his soul should be dealt with as the plate, if he said anything that was false; or, the judgments pronounced in the books of the sages against false testimony, were read, and the witness imprecated those judgments upon himself. I instituted an enquiry among the Chinese, as to whether, among themselves, they had any form of oath that was held specially binding, and learnt that there were certain temples, in which a promise made was held to be sacred. But, in my government at Hong Kong, we abolished the administration of oaths, and made false evidence punishable as perjury. The form of the marriage vow is, however, well described in the text.

spring season, when I first had the fortune to
meet you.   And now the summer is gone and
the autumn is coming.   O, how I prayed to
see the moonlight breaking through the clouds,
—how impatiently I watched,—how long my
loving anxieties endured!   It is said that, to
those who love, the parting of a moment is like
a three years' separation.   But now,—but now
the moonshine brightens the universal world.
You are more lovely than Chang Ngo,—and I
claim from you the whole light of your love!"

Bashfully, and blushing, Yao Sien replied:
" Have I not heard of Cho Wen Kiun?[1]   I am

---

[1] A celebrated beauty of the Han dynasty. She was left a widow
at the age of seventeen, and is handed over to infamy from her allowing
herself to be seduced by the wiles of one of the ministers of the Emperor King. A widow cannot marry again, in China, without the
loss of reputation ; but a young widow, who allows her passions to
obtain mastery over her, is execrated. In the great cities of China,
beautiful arches are often erected by their families in honour of
" chaste widows." Three classes of chaste women are marked out
for special honours, and examples of each are cited in the traditions
of the country.

1st.—Those who sacrifice their lives, in order to escape the violation
of their persons.

2nd.—Those, who, having lost their betrothed husbands before
marriage, make a virgin's vow, and devote themselves to the service
of their parents-in-law.

3rd.—Those whose husbands have died speedily after marriage,
make their widowhood perpetual.

a maiden, who, in my silent retreat, have endeavoured to make myself acquainted with the
teachings of the sages.[1]   To-day, since we have
been together in the garden, I have sworn to
you an oath of fidelity,—but I cannot, for
shame, lift up my head in the presence of the
goddess of chastity.   Are you so infatuated as
to have flung away your paper rolls (exercises),
and set aside your student's lamp? Shall your
whole career be ruined on account of your love
for me?   To prevent this, I listened to your
vows.   I swore an oath to give rest to your
soul.   And now you would invite me to the
perils of unsanctioned passion.   Nay! rather
will I fling this wretched body away, and go
and join the holy ones of ancient days.[2]   Thus,

---

[1] The sages teach that, of the five human relations, those between
husband and wife occupy the first place. There are three thousand
ceremonials, (*Li*) but marriage is the most important of all.—*Chinese
Moral Maxims.*

[2] Commit suicide. The memoirs of illustrious women contain
many examples of self-destruction among girls, as evidence of affection for their lovers, and among wives in the service of their husbands. The Emperor Hiang Yu was so enamoured of his beautiful
wife, Yu Ki, that he neglected his public duties and allowed an
enemy to invade his country, upon which she committed suicide.
The Emperor felt the reproof,—gathered together an immense army,
—marched against the foe,—and carried with him, on his saddle, the

there will be no farther languishing for me, and you can pursue your studies in peace."

Showers of tears fell down Liang's cheeks on hearing these words. They thoroughly drenched his silken sleeves. Speechless, he hid his head among the flowers, and heaved a heavy sigh. At last, he said: "Who could have expected this from you? Would you make my grey headed father wretched for ever? I cannot return to him. I cannot abandon you. Do not condemn me to a daily death."

She answered, compassionately: "Be patient, —be of good courage. If it be predestined, we shall be united at last. We must have no more of these daily flirtations in the garden. Do you fancy that I feel no sympathy with your solicitudes? But we must walk in no forbidden paths. From my youth up, I have never liked the unbecoming talk of foolish and

embalmed head of the lady. When passing a river, his horse got frightened at the reflection of a human head on the water and refused to advance. Hiang, knowing that this was of evil augury, and that he should fall into the hands of the enemy, drowned himself. A pagoda was erected in memory of these events, to which boatmen bring offering, to obtain the favourable auspices of "the beautiful suicide."

intrusive women, busying themselves with matters that do not concern them, and pretending to be the interpreters of young men who have given them no mission to speak on their behalf. You must expect no unbecoming surrender from me. I swear that I had rather you should deprive my body of life,—than my soul of shame. Tarry in patience and in hope. Watch and wait,—in due time the bridal chamber shall be prepared, and we will enter upon the enjoyments of domestic life."

Liang felt the deserved reproof; he had been too impassioned,—too presuming. She withdrew to the shadows of the flowers,—he followed her, and they both sat down. He had obtained forgiveness,—confidence was restored,—and they prattled and laughed together. The fifth watch sounded from the city walls.[1] The waiting-maids suddenly announced that it was time for their mistress to withdraw to her boudoir. It was a terrible announcement, and it is hard to say which shed the heaviest shower of tears; but Liang cried out: " O my beloved! this parting sorrow is the bitterest of all. Do

[1] 3—5 o'clock, A. M.

not forget me in my absence.   Let not your oath be like an atom of dust.   Let messengers[1] bring news of you.   If they tarry long, they will find me still and dead."

Yao Sien was even more sad than he.   Tears dropped upon her rouge box,[2] and she said : " I

[1] Original—" wild geese."   P. P. Thoms traces the references to wild geese as messengers to the following tradition : " That, in the reign of the Emperor Cbau Ti, one of the ministers of state was commissioned as Ambassador to an uncivilised tribe, who, instead of recognising his authority, flung him into prison, where he remained for nineteen years.   In order to conciliate the chief of the barbarians, the Emperor sent a princess to his court, asking for the liberation of the minister,—but the chief affirmed that the minister was dead. The Emperor, being one day shooting in his park, saw a letter fastened to the leg of a wild goose, which proved to be a communi-,cation from the ambassador, informing his master that ho was kept in captivity as a herdsman at Ta Tsi.   When the Emperor informed the barbarians that he had discovered their mendacity, they fancied it must have been through some supernatural intervention ; they asked forgiveness, and restored the minister to his master.—*Chinese Courtship*, p. 115.

[2] Chinese ladies are generally accompanied by boxes and bottles containing paints, cosmetics and perfumes, for the adornment of their persons.   The eye-brows and eye-lashes are painted black, with dark pigment, more or less costly.   The face is covered with an impalpable pearl-powder, which, in the cases of the very opulent and luxurious, is made of small pearls, very finely crushed.   There are various imitations of nacre, and other materials.   The cheeks are rouged,— the lips painted vermilion.   A great variety of perfumes is also employed.   The adorning of a lady's face and chevelure, in China, is a work of far more elaborate art than was exhibited in all the pilings, poomatumings, and paintings of the heads of English ladies in the reign of the early Georges.

shall be hidden behind the crimson screen, and, in my ornamented chamber, will endeavour to dream that the pangs of deferred love are not altogether intolerable. And yet I could not believe that separation would be so sorrowful. But take this as my last and most earnest council,—press it to your heart. Strive for fame,—win it,—that our names may be sooner written upon the scarlet scroll,—that our fore-fathers may see it and rejoice."

They seized one another's hand, and held them as though they could never part. But the cocks were crowing loudly to the cawing of the rooks, and the moon had descended in the western twilight. Liang conducted Yao Sien to her habitation,—four silvery streams fell as they slowly paced along. She entered her boudoir with silent and trembling steps,—he, still more slowly, wended his way to the shadows of the weeping willows. They were, indeed, like two Mandarin ducks[1] beaten about by the wild waves—driven hither and thither, wholly helpless to direct their course.

[1] Yuen and Ying,—the representatives of conjugal felicity.

CHAPTER XXV.

THE PROMISE OF MARRIAGE IN THE BOAT.

LET us leave the lovers for awhile and recount what happened to old Liang on his return back to his birth-place. He had been for many years in the Imperial Cabinet, but he was so constantly occupied with the thought of the home of his fathers, that he applied for, and obtained his pension of retreat, and was allowed to take his leave of the Court, after being crowned with favours from the Emperor. There was also one of the Presidents of the Home Department, Liu, by name, who had been born in the same province of Wu Kiang, and when he found that the old Liang had decided, with all his honours, to retire from the public service, Liu determined to accompany him, and the very next morning asked for an audience, and obtained permission to withdraw. And so they hired, on the river, a two-seated boat for their homeward journey, and they accompanied one another, for they were old friends and fellow citizens. And every evening, when the boats anchored, they met to converse. By day, too, they were much together, with their golden goblets in hand; more and more they talked confidentially to each other, and were, at last, as unreserved as brothers. It is always delightful to renew acquaintance with an ancient friend. And soon, their sons and daughters became the prominent topic of their discourses. Old Liu spoke of his daughter, who had just entered upon the spring time of life. Everybody said she was clever, and perfectly well bred. Old Liang thought he could not choose a more desirable daughter-in-law, so he proposed his son Liang. The student had already acquired a reputation which was not unknown to Liu,—and thus the fathers pledged themselves to one another, and the match was concluded.

And, over the waters, and amidst the sands, the boats made their way.   The great officials[1] safely reached their domiciles,—and fervent was the joy, and loud the rejoicings, with which they were received.

[1] Mr. Meadows' desultory notes on the government and people give a good account of the ranks, duties, and salaries of the different classes of mandarins. A court calendar is annually published at Peking, which contains a biography of the principal functionaries of the State. Hence, the antecedents of the leading personages are generally known, and the different claus are eager to claim relationship with those who have been promoted. The whole population of China is designated by the words *Pe Sing*, the hundred families, or surnames. The number of family names in the Empire is only five or six hundred. As the laws are very severe against marriage between blood relations, the distinctions of race are notably preserved. In a village, it will sometimes happen that, though the personal names, *Ming*, may be many, the clan names, *Sing*, will be very few. Almost every Chinaman is known by both appellations. There is no name, in China, for which there is not a character having a specific meaning.

CHAPTER XXVI.

A MESSENGER COMES TO SUMMON THE YOUNG GENTLEMAN.

OLD Liang made his way to the city wall, and soon reached his home, where smiles of welcome awaited him from his wife.   He had been absent for many years; his appearance was greatly changed,—the bashful young man had become a grey-headed veteran.

My lady immediately despatched a slave[1] to

---

[1] The slavery which exists in China, is mostly of a patriarchal and domestic character. A great number of female children,—particularly those who promise to be beautiful, are saved from infanticide,—purchased by procuresses, and taught music, drawing and other attractive arts, and sold in the open market, either to the money competitors, or to houses of ill-fame. I have seen, paraded through the

Chang Chow, to summon his young master home.

The old gentlemen told the old lady that he had settled an important family affair,—that he

streets, groups of handsome girls richly clad,—all having crushed feet,—a *sine qua non* in the field of rival beauty. In most of the great cities, there are orphan asylums, in which the mortality is frightful ; and, in many cases, a mother prefers flinging her infant into a pond, or into one of the hollow pillars erected for the reception of toothless infants, to placing it in the turnabout of a foundling hospital. The power of a parent over a child is absolute, and infanticide is justified and recommended by many writers on ethics. They say to the mother : "If you know your child is born to a life of long enduring misery and sin, let it suffer only for a moment, and it will escape both." In the Lettres Edifiantes, the Jesuits constantly refer to the multitudes of abandoned children whom they collected in the streets of Peking, and brought to the knowledge of a saving Christian faith. I have been asked by Chinamen, to lend them money, to prevent them from selling their children for the payment of their debts. A great proportion of the children educated by the Catholic nuns in their convents, have been purchased for a small sum of money, or surrendered without condition to the custody of the religious orders. Religious scruples there are none.

The sale of male slaves is generally for a term of years, and is the subject of a formal, written contract between the parent or guardian and the purchaser. I know of no agricultural slaves attached to the soil, and I imagine that the hold of a master upon a male slave, who wished to secure his independence, would be feeble. This is not the case with female slaves, who cannot work out their own emancipation, and, indeed, who are usually such important personages in a household,—as friends and familiars of their mistresses,—that they could scarcely better their condition by change, and, in fact, often occupy the same status as that of the hand-maidens of the scripture patriarchs.

had betrothed their son Liang to the beautiful daughter of Liu, who was a Mandarin, belonging to the Home Department. " A charming girl,—blooming seventeen,—and happily disengaged. Her name is Yu Khing. She is as clever as she is lovely. We settled it all on board the boats."

One servant was hurried off to require the student's immediate presence,—another was sent to the Record Office to obtain the certificate of his birth. The match-maker immediately obeyed a request for his attendance, and he was commissioned to visit old Liu. He arranged an auspicious day for formalizing the betrothals,—and why should any time be lost?

I know not exactly how happy marriages are arranged by destiny, in former days of our existence, but I can tell you what was done by his servants, in consequence of Mr. Liang's commands.

These peremptory commands were obeyed. The servant made his way to the student's chamber, and said to the student: "Sir! I am come to summon you. You must accompany me without delay. Your honoured father returned yesterday to his native city."

Liang, hearing the news of his father's return, hastened to collect his belongings. He took his lute, packed it with his books, and prepared for his departure. And then he went to pay a parting visit to his aunt and his cousin, not forgetting the Yang family. The old gentleman ordered wine to be brought in, and a collation, in which he bade him "Good-speed." During the meal, he said, smilingly, to the student: "I have some news to tell you, that will not be unpleasant to yourself, and which you may communicate to your honoured father. You know something of a daughter of mine. I fancy she is not unacceptable to you, and if you do not think me unworthy, perhaps I might not be unwilling to surrender my daughter to you in marriage."

Liang bowed most reverently,—most delightedly. "I shall obey your commands." His heart overflowed with joy.

CHAPTER XXVII.

LIANG TAKES A SLY FAREWELL UNDER THE SHADOWS OF THE WILLOWS.

He drained the parting glass,—took leave,— and withdrew to his study, thinking of her to whom he was bound by the oath of fidelity. He went into the back garden,—the air was filled with fragrance, and he saw Pi Yue just entering the garden from the farther end. He sprang towards her, and whispered: "I gave you much trouble last evening,—but I treasure up the remembrance of your great goodness. I see not yet how I can sufficiently recompense you for the favours you have done me. My father has obtained leave of absence from the

Court. I am summoned home to welcome him, and I come to bring my greetings to you before I depart. Will you kindly bear my salutations to your lady in the boudoir,—will you invite her to walk into the garden, for I have something pressing on my heart, which I would fain communicate to her?"

And Pi Yue immediately took the message to her mistress in the boudoir: " The student is waiting for you in the garden,—he wants to take leave of you,—this very evening he returns to his native city."

Yao Sien was terribly agitated. " How can this be? We have but just met, and now he would part from me. I will only bestow one word upon him. Why all this delay in sending for the match-maker?" But she went forth into the garden with her maids. The golden lilies trembled under her as she left the elegant boudoir, and they were scarcely seen among the flowers.

But as the two approached,—avoiding the bright sunshine,—Liang flew towards them, over the garden walks, impatient to approach the lovely maiden. Before he could utter a

7 *

word, the anguish of separation overwhelmed him,—but he pressed her hand fervently, and silently conducted her to the very thickest of the willow-shadows.

And, then, though he could hardly speak for his sobbings: "I must leave you, dearest! A dark cloud will be suspended between us. My father has returned home, with the permission of the Court, and I am summoned to meet him. I cannot disobey. There will be two places in the world full of love's woes and wailings. Maiden of mine! give not the bright pearl to any other man. I have only a moment to tell you, that when your honoured father gave me the parting collation, the words dropped from him that he would consent to our espousals. I, too, will busy myself to expedite the match-maker, and our marriage shall be set in order.

"It is vain to mourn over this our separation. Alas! it must be so. Willow twigs cannot hold the youth who is doomed to part from his love."[1]

Yao Sien hung over the student, and wept.

---

[1] Willow branches are associated with the separation of friends. *Vide* note 2 to Chapter XII.

" Something disastrous will happen.   We shall not be united.   My heart is heavy with sorrowful anticipation.   My father has given his consent,—but what will your parents say?   Think well of the oath written on the flowery scroll, and let neither of us be perjured.   But this I swear.   If your father and mother turn a deaf ear to my hopes, I will not be unfaithful.'   I

---

[1] There is a curious tradition, frequently referred to in Chinese romance, explanatory of the different relations existing between the son, the mother, and the husband, to the wife.   It is said, of a mistake in this matter, that " it made Liaou and it marred Liaou."   The first sovereign of the Han dynasty, not having completed that portion of the criminal code, entitled, " Greater and lesser punishments," called in Liaou Ho, to do so.   His manuscript won the highest approbation from the Emperor, and was ordered to be printed.   While copying it for the press, he was summoned by his mother to dinner, as the rice was getting cold.   He was too busy with his work to attend to her,—but having completed it, he heard the call of his wife, and went immediately.   " What have you been about ? " inquired the mother.   " I have been copying the laws respecting greater and lesser punishments."   " And what is the punishment awarded to him who attends to his wife and disobeys his mother ? "   " Beheading ! " was the answer.   The mother repeated the story, as a joke, to the Emperor, who said : " The maker of the law must obey the law," and while he expressed the greatest sympathy for his minister, he directed his decapitation in the public market-place.   The story reminds us of the tyrant of Agrigentum, who burnt Perillus in the brazen bull he had invented, to enable Phalaris to hear the dying agonies of the condemned criminals.— Thom's Lasting Resentment, p. 60.

A somewhat similar story is recorded in the Chinese Annals of

will never marry another. Death is—and has always been the fate of all, and rather than be untrue to thee, I will sleep on the green grass sod which the dews of evening twilight water. Tell me what is passing in your own thoughts. Conceal nothing from me!"

The student held Yao Sien's hand, which he warmly pressed. " Maiden! The gods have witnessed what passed in the garden. If we are not allowed to grow old and grey-headed together, I will abandon my home,—I will sacrifice my hopes,—I will devote myself to you, whom I will never abandon. Life and death will find me alike faithful. You shall never find a falling off of my love. When you return to your chamber, let no distrust or doubt disturb your rest. From the remotest times, true affection has found the means of triumphing over all resistance. Let not your

the Emperor, who having heard of the cruel tortures inflicted by one of his judges, sent a minister to examine into the case, and he invited the "torturer" to a repast, asking him, as if unconcernedly, "What is the best way of eliciting the truth from a criminal?" " Put him," said the judge, "in a vessel of water—apply the fire—and little by little he will be moved to confession." " I will try the experiment," said the minister. The judge was placed in the jar, and the experiment fully carried out.

fair face be clouded with gloom. Do not look pale and grow thin, for my sufferings will only be aggravated by thinking of yours."

And she answered, smilingly: "Keep up a stout heart, Liang! and proceed on your journey. Plague not yourself with sad perplexities. When heaven has said, 'It shall be!' the words endure for ever. Fix your thoughts on the golden list,—mount upwards, ever upwards, on the steps of the exalted ladder, until you reach the highest."[1]

---

[1] It will be seen how the ambition to obtain literary distinction, permeates through the whole of the private and public life in China. This ambition is kindled in the earliest stages of existence, and lingers even among those who are dropping into the grave. No child is too young to enter the competitive hall,—no grey beard too aged,—if they can obtain the needful certificate. There are few men whose condition is more deplorable than that of the poor disappointed candidates,—those who are just able to pass the preliminary examinations and can proceed no farther. They generally occupy some subordinate position,—become scribes—village school-masters —necromancers, or are engaged in other pursuits, for which their always excellent hand-writing, and moderate acquirements may recommend them. In truth, among all the social institutions of China, the literary competitive examinations are, without comparison, the most extensive in their influence, and the most interesting in their details. Their origin is quite lost in the remoteness of antiquity. In the disorganization and anarchy which seem almost a normal condition of that great empire, this educational machinery has often been the only bond which has held the community together. Even where the government has been unable to enforce

They held one another by the hands and by
the sleeves of their garments, little thinking of
the flight of time. But the beautiful light of
the setting sun was dancing through the willow
trees in golden streaks. How could they loosen
themselves from one another? How could
either venture to take a last look—and then
turn away! They spoke of the bright clouds
that are suddenly dispersed,—of the crystal
bowl that is destined to be broken. One, earth-

its authority,—to collect taxes, or to subdue revolt,—the provincial examinations have never experienced more than a temporary
interruption. From the meanest to the mightiest, all take a part
in these literary combats: they are the true representatives of
the popular power, and prevent the creation of any hereditary
aristocracy, as they introduce into the highest seats of authority, the successful candidates who are taken, without exception,
from all ranks of society. I was formerly in communication with
the mandarin,—the Chwang Yuen, who had obtained the very
highest accessible rank. He was a young man, the son of a small
shopkeeper, who sold stationery in an obscure street of Ning Po.
The number of those who, in their primary examinations, have, of
many millions of scholars, obtained certificates for the triennial
examinations, has been estimated at about 120,000. Of these, it is
understood that less than 100 pass into the highest grade, and are
deemed entitled to the Han Lin or doctorial degree. Honours and
dignities are conferred not on the descendants, but on the ancestors
of those who obtain these pre-eminent distinctions, and the homage
paid to the parents and progenitors, and even the remoter relations of
the fortunate victors, is of the most enthusiastic and demonstrative
character.

wards in the north,—the other, heavenwards in the south, should they not perish in their sorrows?[1]

But they hear the voices of men. However hard the parting, the moment for parting is come. They rose up, only to weep. In ten paces, she mounted the five steps to the door-way. She had the heaviness of death upon her, and of the flowers saw nothing but the shadows. Liang dashed his tears away and returned to his study.

---

[1] Heaven is here intended as the representative of the female,— earth, of the male sex. The moral is, that death and sorrow sweep both away.

CHAPTER XXVIII.

OUR STUDENT RETURNS HOME TO VISIT HIS FATHER.

AND having returned to his study, Liang packed up his books and his dagger,[1] and took his passage, gloomy and distressed as he was, on a boat to convey him home. There was a slight beating of the waters against the banks, and the autumnal winds were blowing the leaves into the stream. The sadness of the departing year suited the sadness of his soul.

Having reached his native city, he sprang on shore,—found his parents at home, and there were mutual rejoicings between father and son.

In ancient times, all candidates for competitive examinations wore a dagger.

They had hardly entered the hall, when the old man said: " You will diligently pursue your studies in the library, and this very autumn you must climb the clouds."[1]

And the old lady added: " We have made a charming arrangement for you. We have betrothed you to the daughter of Liu, the President of the department of Home affairs, and as soon as your name is inscribed in the Golden List, the marriage shall be consummated."

The word "marriage" overwhelmed him,— he was silent. In his inmost heart he had treasured his secret love. He bowed to his parents hastily, and with unutterable emotions retreated to his study.

[1] Succeed in your literary contests.

CHAPTER XXIX.

HE TELLS HIS TALE OF SORROW TO THE MOON.

WHAT could he do when seated in his solitary apartment? His misery was at its height, and irrepressible tears rolled over his cheeks. His breath was arrested by his sobs, and he beat his bosom in his wild anguish. "Alas! alas! we were not predestined to one another. The oath I swore in the garden was a worthless oath, and I have betrayed,—I have betrayed the beautiful Yao Sien. Dearest of women! could I have dreamed that I should not have been united to you for ever, would I have mis-led you a single step? But destiny has issued its decree, and my love and my fidelity are shaken to atoms. I call upon heaven,—but I get no answer. I call upon earth,—but earth will not listen. If, with her, I cannot share a coverlet and a pillow, there is no daylight for me,—my life will be sacrificed to my love. Beloved! little can you know how miserable I am."

He stamped the soles of his shoes upon the ground. He wrung his fingers. Ten times he flung himself upon his bed,—ten times he rose up again.

"O wretched! wretched! That bright countenance is turned away. The zephyr breathed, —the moonlight shone for a moment. Both are lost in the dark clouds."

He gathered together his prose compositions and flung them into the water. Odes, verses, songs and poems, he committed to the flames.

"And now, nothing remains for me but to die. What care I now for passing through the three degrees of honour? They are idle, profitless vanities! A handful of rice and a cup of tea are sufficient for the support of life, and if I had all the luxuries of food and drink, to whom could I offer them? How piercingly the

moon looks through the flowers upon the love-
abandoned man! "

And then he poured out his lamentations to
the moon, for the bright goddess had come
in pity from behind the clouds:

" Beautiful lady! And are we never to be
united in this world? How can I ever forget those first love-greetings in the garden?
Was there ever a truer love than ours? How
can my father undo all that has been done?
How can he destroy all hopes of happiness, and
prevent the young phœnixes[1] from being linked
together?

" I am bewildered in this moonlight. I
know not what to think or do. Is my whole
life to be given over to despair? What avail
these flowing tears and these smarting bones?
The moon shines in soft tranquillity,—but I am
agitated and disturbed. Before one shower of
tears is dried, another shower is falling. Apart
from her, cold is my pillow and chilled my
coverlet. Who can occupy the place of my
beloved? Must I repent me of the vows that
rose as high as heaven? All hope is fled.

[1] Fung and Luan.

Around us, the silken curtains will never be
drawn! Alas! alas! that those should be
divided who long to be united. Maiden of
mine! Sister of mine! Beloved Yao Sien!

" The loving pair[1] have been parted and who
shall bring them together again? Who could
have fancied that a heart so warm as mine
should be turned to cold ashes? If I look to
the moon, my tears flow apace, and the sorrows
of separation seem increased a hundredfold.
My grief, since I bade farewell to my beloved
in the garden, is become more and more intolerable. My eyes wander over the wide
heavens, and when I raise my head, I see the
waters are carrying away, eastward, the blossoms of my love, to be lost in the great ocean.
No! we are not to be one. What is there in
the future to hope for,—what is there in the
past to remember? I will resign myself to
die. Were not my tears burning when I
looked on the cold moon? Who can bring
back past pleasures,—pleasures that have fled
for ever? And of my thoughts of love, who

[1] The fabled birds, Yuen and Yeng,—deemed emblems of married
love and fidelity.

shall be the messenger to her? What is life but grass, shaken by the winds and waves?"

Sighing and weeping, and no longer master of himself, he began to curse the gods! "All my labours of love have been scattered. The east wind has smitten the young male and female phœnixes. And now I will sacrifice my life to her, and the moon, upon whom I look, shall witness the sacrifice."

His tears fell in showers. He twisted his fingers in anguish. His soul became like dust. "We cannot be one in life, but who can prevent our becoming one in death,—and I am ready to die. No! she shall never hear that I have consented to any other espousals." Many a dark thought passed through his mind,—but every thought was absorbed in the faithfulness of his affection. And the moon went down, and the night brought the whistling winds. He retreated to his chamber, hoping to find rest. As he threw down his garments, his eyes fell upon the flowery scroll. The ink was fresh which recorded his oath. He seized the scroll,—and wept over it tears of blood.

"Is this memorial of love become a worthless record? Is it not stamped with the truth-fulness of a heart that is true? Resolute as I am, can I resist the parental command? Must I abandon all hopes of a union here, and look to a union hereafter? I will not be ungrateful, —not unforgetful of her. I cannot be linked to another. Life gives me no retreat,—I must find it in death." [1]

[1] An ancient Chinese proverb says : " Life has three intolerable miseries ; one belonging to youth,—one to maturity,—and one to old age. The child who buries his father,—the young man who loses his wife,—the aged man who had no son to perform the sepulchral rites. Better to die, than to be subjected to these calamities.

CHAPTER XXX

YAO SIEN HEARS OF THE BETROTHAL, AND
BLAMES HER CHAMBER-MAID.

LET us, for a short time, leave the student to his silence and his sadness, and see what is passing with the old people of the Yang family. It was the father's birthday, and there was a great gathering of his acquaintances, bringing their congratulations. The student Yao came with the crowd to offer his good wishes, and he perceived Yao Sien in the distance. The house was full of guests, who chatted merrily together, and filled and emptied their golden cups. Old Yang enquired of Yao whether he had any news of his friend Liang, since his return home. " His study chamber is silent and deserted, and no one now regards it. The willow trees are rotting with neglect,—the flowers are all decaying,—everything is left to perish."

Yao answered " I have heard that my brother Liang is betrothed to a lady,—no doubt he must be very busy with preparations for the marriage, and that may account for his absence to-day."

The old man hurriedly inquired, " To whose daughter is he betrothed? And who is the match-maker that has been employed to arrange the marriage?"

The student replied: " My uncle said it was with the Lady Liu, daughter of the President. The matter has been wholly settled by the old people,—they agreed upon a match-maker. He is getting the certificates of birth, and everything is in train."

The old gentleman bit his tongue,—heaved a deep sigh, and said: " The young man is destined to be a distinguished person. Happy he, whose daughter is chosen by a son-in-law who has so brilliant a career before him. She, too, will rank among honoured and illustrious women."   8

Yao Sien was sitting at a table, and these words set her shivering,—it was as if icicles had suddenly filled her ears. She rose hastily up—bowed to her mother, and hurried to her inner chamber. Her heart throbbed violently, —her tears fell like rain. She uttered an imprecation against Liang:

" The faithless one has betrayed me—he has brought desolation to my green spring. Did he not implore me, with tears and sobs, to listen to him,—and now he has given himself to another. Perjured, oath-violating man.[1] I am condemned to hopeless, endless solitude.

" Have not my father and mother applied for

---

[1] The Chinese word for son-in-law is Tan Fou. The literal meaning of which is "flat-paunch." The term dates from the Tsin dynasty, (A. D. 265-419), and is thus accounted for. In those days, Ki Kien sent one of his disciples to select for him a son-in-law, from the family of Wang Tao, who, on receiving the messenger, said : " Go to the outer buildings on the eastern side, and choose one from among my sons and brothers."

The messenger, on returning, said to Ki Kien: " All Wang Tao's young people are handsome, but there was among them one, in the east corner, who lay flat on his belly,—eating gingerbread,—as if he paid no attention to my enquiries." Upon which, Ki Kien cried out, delighted : "That's the man I will have for my son-in-law." And the son-in-law, so selected, turned out to be the illustrious Hi Chi, to whom Ki Kien gave his daughter. A son-in-law has been, from that time, named either Tan Fou—Flat belly, or Tung Chwang, —Eastern bed,—and sometimes the two titles are united.

the register of my birth?[1]   How despicable is
this unloving,—this ungrateful,—this untruthful Liang! To abandon me in a moment,—and
to link himself to another!   O could I, for an
instant, have fancied that his love for me was
so faint and fickle, should I ever so indiscreetly
have opened to him my whole heart in the
garden! Wretched woman that I am!   I am
no mistress of myself.   I must fling myself
into the hands of Yen Kiun."[2]

She wept,—and sighed,—her feelings were
bitterness indeed.

Yun Liang endeavoured to console her.
" My lady! if the student is so faithless as to
break his oath, you should rejoice at being
freed from one so unworthy of you. If he
value not your truth and troth, you too will be
freed from your pledges. A lady, so charming
as you, will not fail to find some deserving
lover. You shall have one more deserving
than this treacherous Liang. Faded leaves
and decayed branches do not become espousals,

---

[1] Have not the authorities been advised of the betrothal, and the
public been made acquainted with it ? The loss of reputation is
attached to the rupture of engagements that have proceeded so far.

[2] See note to Chapter XX.

—nor soiled garments,—only beautiful and spotless gems.[1]

But Yao Sien shouted to her maid: "Flippant, foolish prater! Impertinent and thoughtless creature! Was it not you that lauded him as if he were of embroidered silk? Was it not you who allured the fisher to ford the stream, and now you are lending your idle tongue to tear him away from me? I have studied in the books of the classics all the forms and obligations of vows and oaths, and there is nothing —no, nothing to justify him. Do not all the sages say that, he who has pledged his faith in the betrothal cup, can never be released? Was I not plighted to him in the garden,—and even though he be wanting in virtuous principle, am I to follow his example,—must I believe that his former affection for me has undergone a change? Come what else may,—death will be a relief at last. I am hardened and immoveable."[2]

Pi Yue then came forward with her words of comfort: "But my lady has not heard all

[1] See note to Chapter V.
[2] Literally, "My liver is brass—my gall is iron."

that is to be said in the matter. From the oldest time, espousals have been arranged by parents, and children have nothing to do with their proposals. The story is reported that Liang has been betrothed to the Lady Liu,— but has any one said that Liang has given his consent, and been a party to the betrothal? In your anger, may you not be doing a great injustice? And, at the worst, if you have been deceived, the fault is not yours, and your sorrow is unavailing. At all events, let us talk about pleasant matters, for the spring-tide of youth does not last long."

CHAPTER XXXI.

YAO SIEN DESTROYS THE ORNAMENTS IN HER CHAMBER.

YAO SIEN having listened to the condolences of her maiden, felt that the gushing of new tears filled the channels which had been made by the tears she had shed before. "This intolerable burthen has brought my life to its end. Away, then, with these paintings and adornings,—and foolish dreams and desires. I shall never again stand before my mirror to decorate me. Once, I delighted in these vanities. In this chamber I will destroy them all.'

She threw her rouge and cosmetic box into the pond, that she might show her determination to abandon all care of her pretty face.

"I will not even hope for peace or joy. I will seek my way to the yellow wells,[1] and find forgetfulness there."

And then she took up her luxurious looking-glass and her costly lute, and broke them in pieces. "Who, in the world, cares for my music, now,[2]—who will ever ask me how I look in the mirror? Like a solitary phœnix,—like a lonely swallow,—I shall droop and die."

She threw her jasper flute away,—she tore the strings of her guitar,[3]—but fell weeping like Yu Kwan,[4] whose tears stained her silk garments.

"I would not yield to the entreaties of Lung Yu, himself, nor subject myself to be betrayed

[1] The water, found in graves, is called the yellow springs or wells, and a visit to them is tantamount to an announcement of death.

[2] Chapter XXVII.

[3] The commentator remarks that, Yao Sien had not properly studied ancient history, or she would have known that Chao Kum did not destroy her guitar, (see note to Chap. XXIII.), but pressed it to her bosom. Yao Sien, on the contrary, in order to prevent her lover from entering into another engagement, and to keep him to his oath, broke the strings of her musical instruments. She should not, therefore, have compared herself with the heroine of former days.

[4] Yu Kwan is said to have died of grief, when banished from China, in order that she might marry a Tartar prince,. Wetting, or staining garments with tears, is an ordinary phrase for conveying the image of extreme sorrow.

by a perfidious Liao Chi. I will rather die. A pile of yellow earth shall be my habitation."

She next burnt her many-coloured pencils, and tore up her flowery note paper. "I will write no more poetry,—I will not leave a fragment behind me. I long only to sleep for ever among the flowers."

Next, she burnt her backgammon board, and scattered her draughts over all the chamber. "He has deceived me with treachery and lies! I think on these fleeting moments of hope and bliss with vain regrets. What, though my eyes weep blood,—what, though my sleeves are drenched with tears!"

She seized her harp, and broke it,—her dominoes she flung about on all sides. The sight of anything that had given her pleasure was intolerably painful. "On whom shall I wreak my vengeance? On you, faithless one! on you, be my last curses!"

And then she threw her embroidered silks and satins into the fire.

"What have I now to do with the adornings of the toilet? Never, again, will I gird myself with an ornamented belt. No! I will forget everything. But know you, treacherous Liang, that you are the cause of my destruction."

So, having burnt her garments, she broke her golden nails.[1]

" My ornamented bed is cold and cheerless. There is nothing upon which an unfortunate girl can rely. I am useless and worthless in this wretched world,—and from the world I will withdraw for ever."

She had destroyed all her treasures,—all but one. That was the flowery scroll, on which the betrothal oath was written. She took it up, and it brought to her memory every circumstance that had occurred in the garden. " Yes! I shall die," she quietly said, " die a pure virgin,—a victim of chastity."

---

[1] Chinese ladies of rank allow their nails to grow to the length of several inches, as an evidence that they are never employed in manual labour. They stain them of a golden colour, and at night they are protected with metallic coverings, to prevent their being accidentally broken. To break the long nails, is the last act of despair.

CHAPTER XXXII.

YAO SIEN LEARNS THAT HER FATHER HAS BEEN PROMOTED.

IT is impossible to number the multitudinous thoughts that passed through Yao Sien's mind. Unexpectedly, Li Chun brought her an important message,—that her father had been promoted to be Major-General of the left wing of the army, and commandant of the camp, —that he was to take the earliest opportunity of setting sail, and, with his whole family, to pay a visit to the capital. The news only added to the distress of Yao Sien. "Hopeless before, I am more hopeless now. Never again shall I see my beloved. Heaven has no bounds,

—the way is distant,—mountains and rivers will be between us. This is nothing,—were he not betrothed to Liu! It is decreed,—it is written in the book of heaven that I am condemned to loneliness. To none can I confide the overflowings of my heart."

But she obeyed the commands of her parents, packed up her few belongings, and prepared for the long journey. On an auspicious[1] day, the sail was hoisted, and they prepared for their journey. Water and mountains,—mountains and water, gave no relief to the monotony of her gloomy reflections. What comfort had she in hearing the heavy waves dashing against the boat, as it made its onward way through the dreary landscape! Around her there was nothing but gloom,—and little recked she of the dangers—the ordinary dangers—through which they passed, and managed to surmount. At last, they reached the Imperial residence, and anchored against the city wall.

[1] The choice of an auspicious day for any important undertaking is always a very serious matter in China. The Imperial Almanack, published yearly, under the authority of the Astronomical Board, in Peking, gives a list of lucky and unlucky days, and is habitually consulted.

CHAPTER XXXIII.

OLD MR. YANG HAS HIS FAMILY LODGED IN THE HOUSE OF THE MANDARIN TSIEN.

YANG made all the needful arrangements for the disembarkation of his household. The palace assigned to him was magnificent, — everything was new and well ordered.

On the appointed day, he went to the audience of the Sovereign Lord. There had been many disorders and revolts on the frontiers,[1] and His

---

[1] Disorder, in some part or other of China, is really the normal state of the empire. The authority of the Emperor has never been thoroughly established, and, in many of the provinces, taxes are collecting with great irregularity and difficulty. On the northern and western frontiers, there are whole districts where independent races wholly repudiate the orders which emanate from the Court,— wear the ancient costumes,—retain the chevelure of the time of the

Majesty directed him to take the military command in the disturbed districts, and graciously
said to him: "When you have held your post
for a year, and return to the capital, I shall
know how to appreciate and to reward your
services."

Having received the Imperial instructions,
Yang returned home,—when he poured out
wine, in company with his wife, to whom he
said: "I must hasten to my post,—but I do
not think that you can conveniently return to
your birth-place. But here is a fellow of the
Hanlin College,[1]—his name is Tsien,—he is my
brother-in-law, and your own brother. You
must take our daughter to his house, and abide
with him for a twelvemonth. You will wait
till I return to the Court, or until I am able to
summon you to me. And, thus, I shall have
no anxiety about you, and nobody will meddle
with our affairs."

Ming dynasty, and have not allowed a single Manchoo to settle
among them. The *Meaou Tze*, a wild tribe inhabiting Kwang Si,
sometimes come down to Canton to trade, and are not molested.

[1] The culminating position for the literatis of China, and the
great object of ambition in the succession of competitive examinations.

And so my lady Yang packed up her baggage, hastily, and prepared the parting meal.

When the old man had drank the farewell glass,—he thus conveyed his last wishes to his wife and daughter. "You will make your abode with Tsien, and there, as brother and sister, you may speak of all that passes in your inmost heart. There is, in the back garden, an unoccupied student-chamber, where he may allow his niece and her mother comfortably to dwell." And, to Tsien, he said: "When my mission is completed, and I return to the Court, be assured, my beloved brother-in-law, that I shall find means of rewarding all your kindness." And they took each other by the hand, and parted.

Yang mounted his horse,—brandished his whip, and set forward on his journey. When he reached the frontier, he summoned infantry and cavalry to the garrison. His martial bearing, his activity, his courtesy, won the hearts of the soldiers. He resembles truly an ancient general of the Court.

CHAPTER XXXIV.

LIANG RETURNS TO CHANG CHOW.

WE must leave the General and the frontier, and look into the student chamber. Disappointed in all his hopes, he had become morose and gloomy, and carried on his studies without animation or interest. He often threw aside his books to surrender himself to melancholy thoughts: he sat, despondingly, at his window, and many an unchecked sob burst from his bosom.

"Will she not reproach me with my broken vows, when she hears of this betrothal? How can I inform her that I am not faithless to my first love? To her,—to none can I speak of what oppresses my heart, and ask for sympathy with unuttered and unutterable sorrow. I cannot remain here. I will revisit my study-chamber. I will say farewell to my parents. I will make my way to Chang Chow. I will seek my beloved. She shall know all that is passing within me, and if we wander together into the unseen world, we may be happy."

And he immediately went to the reception hall, where he found his parents, and said to them: "I cannot pursue my studies here, for my heart is not at ease. I am come to take leave of you. I am going to Chang Chow."

His parents answered: "Son! be it as you will. You must devote yourself to your books, —that is the great concern."

He prepared himself for his journey, and embarked on the passage boat. Neither the sight of the waters, nor the hills, gave him any pleasure. He only thought of that bright, happy day, when he had dreamed of lasting union with his beloved;—but now the moon had sunk in darkness,—the flowers were all decayed, and his heart was broken.

But he arrived at Chang Chow, and passed the city wall.

With slow and melancholy steps, he wended his way to his lonely study; casting, as he passed, anxious glances over the flower garden, and fancying that he might have a chance of assuring his beloved of the fidelity of his affection. But, as he moved, his heart grew heavier. He listened, yet he heard nothing but the buzz of winter insects, and the chirping of the goldfinches. As he passed through the more shadowy passages, he observed evidence of the approach of spring. He saw the snowy-white blossoms on the peach trees, and though they seemed to smile upon him, they brought no relief to his sadness. Every old recollection was over-clouded with gloom, and the mournful memory of by-gone pleasures was made all the darker, from the thought that they were departed for ever. He entered the inner garden,—it was a neglected wilderness. The water in the ponds was fetid and stagnant,—covered with green duckweed, that had been allowed to accumulate. The stone bridge looked as if it had never been traversed,—the paths were unweeded. Everything ministered to his despondency. He walked slowly around the garden, and saw nobody but the gardener, who was seated, idling, under the willows.

Liang asked: "Why have the grass and the moss been allowed to choke the path-ways? Why has all this rubbish been allowed to root? Why have not the leaves been swept away? Why are the stone seats and tables covered with dirt and sand?"

The gardener answered, with a laugh: "Why, have you not heard that Mr. Yang has been promoted, and that he is gone, with all his family, to Chang Ngan, to take possession of his post. Who comes to look upon the flowers or the garden, now? I,—and I am very old, —I am the only living soul left."

The words of the gardener added to his distress. His cheeks were wet with tears, and he hastened to conceal himself among the flower-trees. "The hope of seeing her is departed. Waves and mountains separate us a thousand miles from one another. I might as well follow the shadow of a dream." He determined to visit the Cupola. Might she not perchance be there,—but the Cupola had been abandoned. The poetry on the flowery scroll was, however, still stuck to the wall,—but where was she, who had written the responsive verses?

The sight was very painful to him, and he exclaimed: "Who could have thought that heaven would blight all my prospects of happiness? The place recalls every word she uttered, and every word is scattered like dust. And who but I is to be blamed, if the green spring of my beloved has been blasted? And yet I have not broken my faith. My life shall wear itself out in loneliness. No! I will never obey my father. I will be no party to these espousals, and if he will not grant my prayer, I will repair to the yellow waters, and there I will await the coming of my beloved."[1]

He walked forward into the Cupola. "It was here I swore fealty to her I love. It was here the record was written that we would be eternally faithful. She is far, far away, and has left no trace of her footsteps. We shall not meet again. Turn where I will, all is darkness and death. No happy home on earth will ever be mine."

[1] I will commit suicide, and in my grave expect to be united with her.

He was exhausted by his sorrows, and fell, as if lifeless, on the floor.

The gardener entered the Cupola, and found him stretched like a corpse. He cried out loudly for assistance. The servants and slaves of Liang rushed in confusion and consternation to the spot, but nobody could explain the cause of the catastrophe. They administered to him the life-elixir pills,[1] which restored his lost senses. He said nothing, but sighed heavily. The servants dared to make no enquiries, but they carried him safely to the study chamber, and laid him on his ivory bed,[2] and he whispered: "O, heaven! thou hast pronounced thyself against the five elements!"[3]

---

[1] The Chinese attribute great restorative virtues to certain pills, which are covered with bees' wax to protect them from the influence of the external air.

[2] Bedsteads, in China, are frequently veneered with ivory.

[3] The Woo Hang, or five elements, are metal, water, wood, fire and earth; of these, in three various proportions the life of the human being is composed, and they must be studied for the horoscope of every individual. Death is the dissolution of the Woo Hang.

CHAPTER XXXV.

YAO SIEN HEARS THAT HER FATHER IS BE-LEAGUERED.

WE must leave Liang in his study, and learn what the old Mandarin, Tsien, reported to his sister. " A courier is arrived from the frontier, bringing the news that a hundred thousand accursed rebel soldiers have attacked your honoured husband, and that he is besieged in the border city, and the siege is so closely · pressed, that not a needle can make its way.[1]   I

---

[1] The penalty of death is generally attached to the non-success of any Commander-in-Chief of the Chinese forces. The orders are to subjugate the foe,—and disobedience to Imperial orders is a capital crime.

know not when the rebels will be tranquillized,[1] nor when your husband may be expected home."

Lady Yang was deeply affected by this sad news, and went to her daughter's chamber to communicate it to Yao Sien, who, when she heard it, covered her face with her hands, and almost sank down with grief. " Curses upon these rebel slaves! Why were they not annihilated by the Imperial troops? But what can girls know of such matters? We are not able to save our fathers, and bring them back safely to their birth-place. Alas! that I should be alone, without the blessing of a brother! In vain should I offer to sacrifice myself, in order to save my father. When shall the misery be over, with which he has to struggle, on the frontier? Why cannot I give to my honoured, grey-headed father, some evidence of my affection and my gratitude? "

Lady Yang left her daughter, who continued to pour out the expressions of her sorrow, when there was no one to listen: " I have no

---

[1] The system of tranquillizing or conciliating rebels is a part of the ordinary policy of China. If the leader of a revolt is too strong for subjection, he is bought off either by money or by appointment to some lucrative office.

lover to sympathise with me, and to lighten the burthen of my woes. My father is beleaguered, my life as brittle as paper. Anxiety upon anxiety,—disaster upon disaster! Tears ever flowing, which will never be dried. Under what fatal horoscope was I born? What were my sins in my former existence, to be so heavily punished in this? The sages have wisely said, that: ' to be beautiful, is to be wretched.' Alas! I must break away from life, and return to the yellow earth. But how should my spirit find repose, if I abandon my mother, — leaving her friendless and alone? And, perhaps, my father may yet return to his native city. If he die, who shall perform the funeral rites,—who shall carry the fragrant lamp to his grave? Wretched as I am,—I must live, and the world shall know that, in his death, I did not abandon my father!"[1]

---

[1] No misery or disgrace is held to be greater than that a parent should leave no child to present the funeral oblations at his grave. Hence, the passionate desire to have a son and successor is universal in China. Indeed, the moralists teach it as a peremptory duty of any childless wife to assist in providing a young concubine whose off-spring may render proper services to the manes of the departed. When there is no son, a daughter or a step-son is expected to bring the odoriferous oil lamp to the grave. If there be only one descendant, as in the case of Yao Sien, suicide would be deemed a fearful sin, as the funereal ceremonies could not be becomingly performed, and the spirit would be condemned to be a wandering ghost, for whom there is no rest in the tomb.

CHAPTER XXXVI.

THE STUDENT FINDS COURAGE TO PRESENT HIMSELF FOR A COMPETITIVE EXAMINATION.

WE must leave the daughter bewailing the wretched fate of her father, and visit the student in his chamber, where he was placed, exhausted, upon a sick bed. Many a day he passed, wearied and weeping over his forlorn fate. He pined through the whole spring-season, and when summer came, it brought him no consolation,—he could not rid himself of his melancholy thoughts, nor help dreaming of his beloved. One morning, his cousin Yao came to see him in his study, and to inquire about the state of his health.

"The examiner is coming," said Yao, "and you must go in and mount up the ladder,—and you must mount high. You must busily read your books, and study the annals. Of what avail is it, to waste your days with frowning eye-brows? Rouse yourself. Tell me what you are doing. Nothing is so mischievous as secrecy and gloom."

But Liang dared not tell his cousin the true state of matters. If he did, it would ·bitterly wound him. So he quietly answered: "Dear cousin! listen for a moment. Where can I find spirits to pursue my studies? I shall fail, —I cannot be promoted. Did ever a sick man succeed?" Yao responded: "You have great talents,—they will bring you success and glory. You will ride upon the neck of the whale, you will be close to the Chwang Yuen."[1] "No!"

[1] When in China, I received an autograph communication from the Chwang Yuen, who stood at the head of all who had passed the literary examinations of the year. Now, when it is considered that there are probably not less than thirty millions of children in the village or primary schools,—that, of these, not more than one hundred and thirty thousand pass to the first examinations, and, of these again, only about one-tenth, say thirteen hundred, pass to the second rank,—and that the Chwang Yuen, is the first of the thirteen hundred, it will be seen what his position must be, in a country where literary pre-eminence is the great object of ambition. In the case

9

answered Liang: "but I am hopeless. I am not fit for competition. I am sinking. My wretched life will terminate before the arrival of another spring."

Yao laughingly replied: "Nay, cousin of mine! You talk like a demented man. I know you to be a clever fellow, who can conquer difficulties, and succeed if he will. Now, I am sure there is something on your mind that you have not communicated to me,—some secret sorrow. You say you will not venture into the competitive struggles. Are your ten

mentioned, the Chwang Yuen was the son of a person who kept a small stationer's shop, in an obscure street, at Ningpo,—his forefathers, as a matter of course, were crowned with titles; for, in China, hereditary honours do not descend to children, but ascend to parents and forefathers,—and all the influential people in the district, as well as the highest functionaries, personally presented themselves, to congratulate the family on the distinction they had obtained through the merits of their son. The meaning of Chwang Yuen is " adorned head,"—the head being garlanded with flowers when the announcement is made of his success. I would mention here, in reference to the great neglect of good writing, and sometimes even of correct spelling, in many of our educational establishments, that any inattention to the perfect formation of the Chinese characters, in the exercises submitted to the competitive examinations, would be altogether fatal to the success of the student. It were well if a little more regard were paid to this matter in our own country, in which the cacography of many of our young men is disgraceful alike to their tutors and to themselves.

years of study to be thrown away? The triennial examinations are at hand. Lives there a
man who does not long to walk upon the azure
clouds? You have not had the stupendous
adversity of seeing your name excluded from
the lists. Listen to my counsels. Surrender
not yourself to listlessness and dreariness.
Think of your father,—and of the misery you
may cause to him. Remember that, from the
oldest times, we have been taught that it is the
very first of our duties to obey and to honour
our parents, and he must be a fool—or worse—
who neglects to do so."

Yao could have employed no arguments
more irresistible. Moreover, the thought of
his beloved gave additional force to Yao's
words. His determination was taken. He
would visit the capital,—he would pursue his
studies. Yao left him with friendly salutations.
Soon after, it was announced that the Imperial
examiner would hold his sittings. So the two
students determined to take leave of their
parents, and to hasten to the metropolis.

CHAPTER XXXVII.

LIANG packed up his travelling gear, and made his way to his native city. He saluted his parents,—returned to his study,—and devoted himself to the reading of the classics and the chronicles.

The autumnal winds were summoning the youths to their examinations. Liang went to the family hall, to take leave of both his parents.

Father and mother gave him their last exhortations. " Be careful in all you do, and separate not yourself from your cousin. Be diligent in your studies, and steadily pursue them on your voyage. Be not enticed by the flowers and willows[1] of the capital, and when you have the good fortune to be placed on the tiger-board, be not impatient to bring home the news, but wait in the capital, and strive to be placed in the highest ranks. Persevere, and mount, step after step, higher into the azure clouds of heaven."[2]

Having received their blessing, he embarked for Chang Chow, in order to accompany his cousin Yao, who took leave of his mother, and they departed together. Up went the sails, and forward the boat on the river. The land-scapes on the banks were beautiful, but they had other work to do than to be admiring hills or rivers. They were little encumbered with travelling trunks, and, at last, they safely reached the capital.[3]

[1] Profligate women.

[2] The names of those who are elected to the second grade of Master or Kiu Jen, is published on Tiger-day, the ninth of the ninth moon. Hence, the list is called the Tiger Board,—the Golden Board,—the Yellow Board. The lower grade corresponding to our Bachelor degree, are the Siu Tsai.

[3] As popular education is so frequently referred to in this novel, and the question of elementary instruction now occupies so much of the public attention in this country, it may not be intrusive here to speak of that remarkable book, the San Tze Ching, or Trimetrical

classic, which, written in the 5th century, is used in every primary
school in the Chinese empire, and in which, probably, not a single
character has undergone either a change of form or of sound in the
last thirteen hundred years. The lines are intoned by the teacher,
and repeated in chorus by the whole of the scholars, laying an emphatic accent on the last word, thus :

Tan chi *tsu*	. .	Men at birth,
Sing pun *shen* .	.	Life-fount good,
Ling siang *chin*.	.	All alike ;
Si siang *yuen* .	.	Then all far.

which Dr. Bridgman translates : " Men at their birth are in nature
pure.   In this, all are alike, but in practice they differ."

The book consists of 346 lines, or 1068 words, representing about
500 characters ; these are universally known, and are sufficient for
the ordinary business of life. A tolerably instructed man is supposed
to know from four to five thousand, which is only about one-tenth
of the whole number which covers the literary field.   Kang Hi's
Dictionary, of which the common edition consists of 21 volumes, has
about 22,000 characters.   The great Thesaurus of characters and
sound occupied seventy-six learned men, under the reign of the
great Kang Hi, for eight years, and comprises 130 thick volumes,
printed at the public expense, in 1711. (*Callery Sys. Phon : part I.*)

Thus, the book begins by asserting the purity of childhood, and
that neglected education is the cause of the deterioration of man.

The third and fourth lines are a maxim of Confucius, having the
condensed antithetical character of most of his teachings, of which
the more elaborate meaning is : " that men all resemble one another
by their common nature ; but all become different from one another
by pursuing different courses." The fifth and sixth lines :—" Life un-
taught, Nature droops ; (in) teachings path, first is toil," may be literally translated : " Suppose no teaching, nature is deteriorated." The
seventh and eighth, " (In) Education's path, noble (most important)
is application."   Then, examples are given of the good conduct of
Mencius and Lao Tze, and the poem continues :—

Youth untrained	.	.	Gem unwrought,
Father's fault .	.	.	Gives no light ;
Teach, no rod—	.	.	Man untaught,
Master bad : .	.	.	Knows not right.

Child not learn— . .	Man a child,
Must not be ; . .	Tender age ;
Not learn young, . .	Teacher, friends,
What when old ? . .	Manners learn.

Or, " If a child is uneducated it is the fault of the fathers; and if in teaching there be no punishment, it is by the neglect of the master. It is most improper that the child should not learn, and if he learn not when young, how can he when he is old ? " Then follows a quotation from the Book of Changes. " The unwrought gem is a useless article ; the unlearned man knows nothing." " A man, when a child, being of tender (susceptible) age, should, by his teachers and friends, be taught politeness."

Here, again, examples are given in illustration. Then the social duties are enforced, then the decimal system :—

Powers are three— .	Lights are three—
Heaven, earth, man ; .	Sun, moon, stars. .

The four seasons, the cardinal points, the five elements—water, fire, wood, metal, earth ; the five virtues—benevolence, justice, propriety, wisdom, truth; six kinds of grain for man's food, six species of animals for his service ; seven passions which move him,—joy, anger, sorrow, fear, love, hatred, and desire ; eight musical instruments, nine degrees of kindred ; rules of precedence, the ten duties which every teacher should clearly point out; a description of the writings of Confucius, Mencius, Tsz'sz, and Tsang ; first the four books, then the six classics,—other books are also recommended. Next come the Imperial and ministerial laws,—instructions, injunctions, vows, and mandates ; character of the Chinese government,—the ritual, national music, odes, the annals, commentaries after the classics, the philosophers, important parts to be committed to memory, and concludes by study of general history.

Such is the broad outline of the most important book employed in China for initiating education. It is the synopsis of the Chinese curriculum. Being rhythmical, it is easily retained in the memory, and, from constant repetition, it is so engraven in the mind of every child, that, if two or three words are quoted from any portions of it, he will go on repeating what follows, like a clock running down.

CHAPTER XXXVIII.

HEAVEN REVEALS THE GOOD FORTUNE OF THE STUDENTS.

ON reaching Nan King,[1] they hired a neat, but

[1] Late newspapers from China give some interesting particulars of the resumption of competitive examinations in Nan King, where they had been long interrupted by the presence of the Tae Ping insurgents. An Imperial decree directed the examination hall to be opened in the ancient capital of China. No less than two thousand students presented themselves as candidates for the Kiu Jen, or Master of Arts degree, and in consequence of the time which had passed since the last examination, an unusual number, not less than 248 students, were promoted. So severe was the competition, that great numbers committed suicide, and many others died from over exhaustion and anxiety. It is said that, no less than 75 corpses were carried out from the examination halls. They were removed by secret, underground passages, lest the great entrance should be profaned by the presence of the unhappy dead, who are supposed to pay this most awful penalty for undivulged offences, which ought to have prevented them from entering into the competitive field.

simple chamber for their abode. They passed through their courses of examination in the halls, and returned home with satisfaction and gladness, and when the list of the successful candidates was published, the name of Liang —O, joy of joys! appeared as promoted to the rank of Kuai Yuen,[1] and the name of Yao stood the thirtieth in the golden list. Messengers were immediately dispatched to their families, announcing the auspicious event. After the festival of honour[2] was over, they

Perhaps, in the whole administration of China, the least corrupt is the educational department. The Imperial examiners have frequently been beheaded for acts of favouritism, but, notwithstanding this severity, it is believed that, about one tenth of the successful candidates obtain their promotion by bribery, or by other unwarrantable influences.

[1] The first place among the Kiu Jen.

[2] When the examinations are over, the list of the promoted is hung up in the Palace of the Governor of the Province, and saluted with three salvos of artillery. The Governor presents him, and bows before the list, and a second discharge of artillery takes place. A few days after this, " the promoted" are invited by the Governor and the high provincial authorities, to a feast of honour in the palace. They are served by all the subordinate functionaries, and two youths, fantastically attired, hold olive branches over the heads of "the promoted." The festival is called Lu Ming Yen—" Stag Shouting Festival," from an old tradition that, when the stag hears certain joyful songs, he breaks out into cries or shouts. The Emperor also gives a feast, called the "Jewel-forest Feast." To it, the greatest literary celebrities are invited, who are compared to a forest of precious stones.—*Schlegel*, p. 99.

hired a boat, and embarked on the river. Then thought the Kuai Yuen of his beloved Yao Sien, with globular tears, in which sadness was mingled with delight.

" And, now, were it but my happiness to be united to my beloved, I should enjoy an ever-lasting spring-time of fame and honour. To-day, is my name pronounced as worthy of note, still, I cannot see the blue waters,—nor the green hills,—for my thoughts are concentrated on her who is absent."

But he concealed his anxieties, fearing that Yao might perplex him with inquiries. When he was alone, he gave way to his emotions, and at night, his dreams were filled with images of his mistress. So absorbed was he with his many reflections, that he scarcely noticed that the boat had reached the end of the voyage, and anchored at the city wall.

The first enquiries Liang made were about the Yang family, and he was informed that the Major-General had been sent to the frontiers, and was there beleaguered by the accursed rebels. Nobody knew what had become of his daughter, and it would be very difficult to discover where she was. Sorrowful, indeed, was this information to Liang.

"What can I do to find my beloved? Between us are clouds of dust and stormy winds, and I know not whether she is alive or dead. Where can I seek her? Why did we ever separate? Have I not met her love with ingratitude? What care I for fame? I will not proceed farther with these examinations."

But Yao gave him better councils, and encouraged him to enter again into the competitive field. The list of the conquering candidates was proclaimed. Liang's name was the eighth. Yao's was in the middle. They were taken to be examined on the golden steps,[1] and, on the day when the Son of heaven addressed the students, Liang was raised to the third grade.[2] Yao obtained the first grade in the second class.[3] The Emperor graciously invited them to the Jewel-forest Feast. Yao

[1] In the presence of the Emperor.

[2] The third on the list of the Han Lin (Doctors) bears the title of Than Hwa,—"the flower seeker." The second is the Pang Yen, "Accepted graduates eyes." For the highest, the Chwang Yuen, "the ornamented head."—See p. 193.

[3] A Tsin Tze.

was appointed to an office in the Ministry of the Home Department, and Liang was named a member of the Han Lin College, and took his seat in that distinguished place.

A beautiful palace was appointed for his residence,—a stud of fine horses was given him and he was called to the service of the Court. There was a noble park behind his palace, and, after the evening twilight, it was his delight to walk in the moonshine, and to look upon the fragrant flowers.[1]

---

[1] Evidence of his fidelity to his mistress.

CHAPTER XXXIX.

THE ACADEMICIAN AGAIN ENCOUNTERS HIS BELOVED.

LEAVE we the academician to his repose, and let us visit the sorrowful lady. She had heard of the straits in which her father was placed, and it was a heavy, additional burthen upon her already too sorely oppressed heart. She sighed over the melancholy condition of the love-lorn. "And he," she said, "has doomed me to sit for ever by my lonely lamp." Yun Liang and Pi Yue, when they saw their mistress' grief, invited her to walk in the garden. So she slowly raised her golden lilies, and, as the door of the garden was opened, she entered, accompanied by her maids. And they wandered among the flowers, while she cast anxious glances around. Beautiful she was, but her very shadow showed that she was the victim of melancholy. Her head drooped, when she called to mind the events of the past year, and tears, which she could not restrain, moistened the sleeves of her silken garments.

"Well do I remember the spot where I met him! The bright full moon smiled upon us—sanctioned our union,—with my whole heart I felt that we were pledged to each other, and who could have thought that our hopes were to be blasted? Where is he, from whom that weeping separation, under the willows, took place? Not a word have I heard about him,—and there can be no doubt he has broken the oath which he swore under the flowers. If we meet in the street, it will be as mere chance passengers. From none of them could I seek solace for my sorrows. My beauty is departed,—my spirits sink when I think of him. I have seen the peach blossoms blown away by the winds of spring. They are carried off by the stream, or scattered over the flat roofs. Who will condole with the bitter thoughts of this evening?"

And then, sobbing, she turned to the moon, but only to think of him who was so far away.

Who could have fancied that Liang's house was just on the other side of the wall? And he, too, was there, and heard the sweet sounds, that were brought to him by the soft breeze. He listened, and said:

"What is that heavenly voice which I hear among the flowers? It is the song of the mango-bird, when he flies through the branches. It is the moon-goddess speaking in her palace, and lamenting that she is in Kwang Hang, deserted and lonely." [1]

He wandered over the garden, endeavouring to discover the spot whence the sounds had proceeded. Yet he saw nothing but dreaming herons and sleeping flowers,—there was no trace of man. There were bright clouds floating over the distant hills, light as the silk-worms' threads, and, in the ponds, the gold-fish were quietly disporting.

Again, he heard the voice,—but saw not the

[1] Notes to Chapter VI.

speaker.   The wind shook his silken robe, and he seated himself under the willows.

"Somebody, surely," said he, "must be wandering in the garden!"

He mounted the rock-work[1] by the side of the pond, that he might look over the garden, and saw, in the distance, a maiden, whom he could, at first, hardly distinguish from the flowers, and he remarked that the silk sleeves of her robe were wet with tears.   He fancied there was a resemblance to Yao Sien, but could she have become so thin and pale!   He saw that her shadow was lessened,—her dress was simple,—and she stood like a modest statue in the wind.   She looked around, and he was touched with the sorrowful expression of her countenance.

There were two serving girls in the summer pavilion, and he noticed that they were smiling, and pointed to the moon as it peeped through the dispersing clouds.

They were, indeed, the two chamber-maids, Yun Liang and Pi Yue.

[1] The fish ponds which ornament the gardens of the Chinese are generally walled round with rock-work, in whose interstices shrubs and flowers are planted.

" It must be the beloved one," he exclaimed. " What can have brought her here?"

And he thought, shudderingly, of the events of the past year,—he could hardly support himself as they passed before his memory.

" Mine is an accursed fate. Our hair will grow grey, and we shall not be united. My oaths, high as the hills and deep as the ocean, are scattered like dust. Could I have foreseen this, never would I have allowed myself to be so entangled in the perplexities of love! How can I scale the high wall that separates us? Yet it would be cowardly and foolish to turn away, now that I have discovered her. I will approach her. I will speak to her. What care I for these seven feet of clay.[1] May I not risk my life, in order to be united to my beloved?"

And he suddenly sprang over the wall, and fell among the flowers. Yao Sien shrieked out,—her heart trembled.

She called out to her chamber-maids to see what had happened. The timorous Yun Liang beckoned to Pi Yue, who shouted: " What thief is that, who dares to frighten the chamber-maids?"

---

[1] My body.

Liang made a low bow. "Fair ladies! Can it be that you have forgotten Liang? A whole spring has passed since I met you among the flowers."

The moonlight enabled Yun Liang to see that it was no other than Liang, and she knew that it was his voice to which she had been listening, so she hurried away to her mistress to tell her the news.

So the lovers met,—met with overflowing tears,—and the sleeves of their silk garments were bedewed.

Yet they were speechless. What words could express their feelings? Yun Liang and Pi Yue were equally moved. At last, Liang dried his tears, and said: "I was separated from you by a heavy mountain of sorrow. It was covered with clouds and storms. I was torn by a hundred miseries when, last year, I parted from you to return to my home. And now I have the bliss of looking again upon your lovely countenance, and I will repeat the vows of my unchanged love."

Yao Sien answered, sorrowfully:

"The distinguished man is no longer what

he was,—and honoured as you are, you may claim a bride from the goddess of the moon.[1] It is sad, indeed, that our hopes should be scattered to dust. Where is the oath now, which you swore amidst the flowers? Liang! you are truly an ungrateful man. I once fancied that there was faithfulness in the world, and little thought you would be found among the unfaithful and the unloving. Thanks to you, I am condemned to loneliness,—but when I am hidden behind the curtains of my chamber, will your heart be at rest? Can you, who have destroyed the happiness of my life, find comfort for your own? I scarcely believe that the pure heaven will look complacently upon the untruthful. I know I am only a poor girl, yet I value truth and honour more than a thousand pieces of gold, and if I am not your wife, I will consecrate myself to the flower goddess who recorded the history of our love. I heard you had been betrothed to Liu's daughter, and I gave all my belongings to the flames.

"And now will I resign myself to my soli-

[1] *i.e.*,—I am unworthy to be the wife of one who has been elevated to such honour.

tude,—for it would break my heart to think of any other alliance. I have had the fortune of meeting you once more, and of telling you all, and now I am ready to die, and to wait for you in another world.

" Think not of me when your marriage rites are celebrated. Be happy in the embraces of another woman. I know that the new flower is more fragrant than the old. You will forget her, to whom you pledged your faith,—upon whom the bright moon shines upon the green hillock, but whether for her, you will not care to ask. Is it her doom to envy another?"

She uttered these words in a soft, sweet tone, but her tears stopped her farther utterance. She leaned mournfully on the balustrade, and her spirits sank. The dim moon,— the silent flowers,—the stifled buzz of the insects, were the sole but fitting companions of the abandoned one. Yet there was another being not less distressed than herself. The grief,—the misery of both are not to be described.

At last, Liang found a voice. " I humbly implore you, fair lady! to listen to what I have

to say. Why should you do me the injustice
of supposing that I have forgotten your kindness and your promises? The difficulties in
the way of marriage are not the work of man.
How often have I desired to convey to you the
feelings of my soul, but I could find no way
of passing to you over the blue bridge. Heaven
and earth have taken pity upon us,—and now
we meet,—and though heart-broken I will tell
you all.

"After I had taken leave of you last year,
and returned to my native city, I found that
my parents had contracted a marriage engagement for me. I dared not inform them of my
secret affection, but concealed a sorrow which
was likely to destroy my life. I had nearly
determined to seek you out, and to confide to
you all my cares, and longed for death as my
sole relief.

"I returned to the way which leads to the
celestial terrace.[1] I heard that your father
had been promoted, and had been summoned
to the capital, and therefore did not find my
beloved in the back garden. Such was my

---

[1] The Lady's garden.

distress, that I swooned in the summer-house. Thanks to the gardener who found me, and brought the needful help, I was restored to life.

"I had no courage to seek for honour or for glory, but my cousin Yao counselled me with much earnestness not to abandon my studies, but to go in to the triennial examinations, and struggle for the highest rank. I then went to the capital specially in search of you, and there I heard that your honoured father´ was be-leaguered by the rebels .Thus, mists and rain, clouds and mountains, separated me from my beloved, and I began to think that my life was worthless as an autumnal leaf,—for whichever way I turned, I could learn nothing of you.

"Since then, sickness and sadness have taken possession of me,' and I scarcely retain the like-ness of man. In the cold, I forgot to clothe myself, and, though hungry, I did not care to eat. It was all wretchedness, from the rise of the morning to the twilight fall of evening. I knew that my earthly career would soon be closed, and of my many gloomy thoughts, the gloomiest was that I had made you unhappy.

¹ I am white as the Mei flower.

But I persevered with my studies, and my name stands on the golden list. I was announced as one of the selected for the flowery garland.

"And now the moon is at its full,—and we have met again. Is our meeting anything but a dream?

"I beseech you to tell me, from the beginning, what has brought you here to dwell?"

Yao Sien, after sighing deeply, said: "What could induce me to believe that you had not forgotten my love? I know, now, that the blame belongs to your parents, and how can you induce them to change their plans?

"But it is the will of heaven, and not that of man, which settles all events. Was the link between us, in the former world, so weak, that it must be broken in this?[1] for the moon has looked down coldly upon us,—the blossoms are scattered, and we cannot be one. A west wind and a heavy rain have torn the intertwined branches asunder, and we are delivered over to a boundless misery.

[1] The Chinese, who believe that "marriages are made in heaven," say that the predestination belongs to a former state of existence, and that the consummation takes place in the present stage.

"When my father went to the borders, I could not remain at home, but went with my mother to dwell with an academician. He is an uncle of mine on the mother's side, and his name is Tsien. For me, I am like the weeds which are driven on the surface of the water—over lakes and seas—now floating, and now sinking.

"Of my father, I have no news from the other side of the great wall. I know not whether he is alive or dead. He was a thousand miles away in the frontier town.

"And, to-day, Sir! I have the bliss of meeting you,—but our meeting is in a strange city. I doubted, till to-day, whether I should ever see you again, and thought the chill moon would soon be looking down on my solitary grave."

To which Liang replied: "Lady Yao Sien! My life is like an autumnal cloud, and I had rather perish on the sandy waste,[1] and repay your kindness by the sacrifice by my life, than be unthankful or untruthful to you. I will seize the three-feet long dragon-pool-sword,[2]

[1] The wilderness of Sha Mo.
[2] The twisted, flaming sword of victory. It is supposed to typify the crooked movements of a dragon in a pool.

and destroy the accursed rebels, and thus prove my gratitude to you. I will rescue your honoured father, and bring him safely back to his native city. And when I have rendered this service, I shall be ennobled, and perhaps he will consent to our espousals,—and if I fail to redeem him, I can die upon the battle field, for such a death will not be unwelcome to me.[1] Most beloved of beloved women! You have read the books of the classics,—you have studied our history. We will be true to one another, and the world shall hear of our fame."

A tear of pleasure dropped from the eye-lids of Yao Sien. "Now, I know that your love and fidelity are as deep as the ocean, and mine as firm as metal or rock. The goddess of flowers will acknowledge the sincerity of our hearts."

And they talked over their disappointments and their difficulties. The shadows of the flowers showed that the night was near. They looked up to the moon, and held one another by the hand. But the fainting stars began to give

---

[1] The ancient annals of China are full of records of self-sacrifice to love and to duty, and no appeal could be stronger or more complimentary than this.

notice to the moon that it should disappear, and soon the crowing of the cocks announced that it was time to separate, and they heard the voices of Yun Liang and Pi Yue, summon- them to depart. "The people are awaking," they said, "and putting on their garments. You must leave now, and arrange for another meeting, or you will be disturbed by the ser- vants."

Yao Sien wept again, and said: "I know not when we may meet. Do not hanker after the enjoyment of the clouds of Wu,[1] and let not the night be hateful to me!"

Liang checked his tears, but sobbed heavily, and said: "Beautiful one! have you not yet read my heart? We must separate now—but not to meet again is the doom of death."

And they sought, together, the shadows of the flowers, holding each other by the hand and sleeve. They said: "Would it not have been happiness had we never met? Then we could not have loved one another, nor would our dreams have been so dreary. Alas! that a pitiless sword should sever our affections!

[1] Note to Chapter VI.

If we are to be apart, what matter it whether it be but a step or a thousand miles?"

They heard the birds sing,—they saw the blossoms blown about by the breeze, yet thought of nothing but their own grief; hanging down their heads, they both departed to their homes.

CHAPTER XL.

ON Liang's return to his study-chamber, he sat down by the lamp-light to prepare a memorial, that he might be allowed to proceed to the frontier, to attack the accursed rebels, and to give peace to the land. He desired, in this way, to testify his gratitude for the favours with which Imperial goodness had honoured him. And he clothed himself in his gala garments, and sought an audience from the Son of heaven.

The Emperor was much rejoiced when he read the memorial. " That this youth should offer to proceed to the overthrow of the accursed rebels, is it not an opprobrium to my do-nothing courtiers? But if you succeed in giving peace to the land, I will raise you in the ranks of the nobility, and my rewards shall not be parsimoniously bestowed upon your exalted person."

And the Emperor gave him the sword of dukedom, and directed that a hundred thousand soldiers should accompany him to the borders. Having received the mandates of the Supreme Ruler, he took leave of His Majesty, and was invited by all the courtiers, great and small, to a parting collation. When the festival was over, he mounted his horse, and departed. Columns of sand, blown about by the winds, frequently darkened his path. Often looking round, he could not perceive a living soul in all the wide waste. But he was ready, for his beloved one, to sacrifice his life on the battle field.

We know not yet whether he is destined to live or die,—for it is heaven alone that disposes of all the vicissitudes of defeat and victory.

CHAPTER XLI.

As soon as he reached the borders he prepared for the fight. He sent a message to the governor of the frontier fortress, directing him to expedite auxiliary forces, in order, at once, to annihilate the rebels. The messenger hurried off without delay.

Liang meditated gloomily: " The mountain paths are steep and rough, and my soldiers are little accustomed to them. I must so manage that the rebels may not know that the Imperial troops are coming to attack them. It is an old maxim that "you should pounce upon the enemy when he is unprepared." Meanwhile, many of the robber chiefs pressed upon him. He mounted his horse, in order to overthrow the rebels.   He had not reckoned on the cowardice of the Chinese soldiers, who fled to save their lives.   The rebels took advantage of their poltroonery, followed, and destroyed multitudes of them,—leaving only a few thousand men under Liang's command.   Not knowing the plans of the rebels, he retreated into the mountains, to avoid farther disaster.   He thought he might find some means of escape, but the rebels cut off his passage.

It is an old military saying, that: " The few cannot resist the many."   He saw no chance of safety, and, in the unknown mountain passes, where he was beleaguered, hero though he was, the chances were sadly against him.

Happily for him, he was intrepid, cautious, and persistent, so that the rebels were unable to reach his person, though they surrounded him with some thousands of cavalry and infantry.   They spread a false report that he had been killed, and invited his troops to surrender themselves.

The report reached the capital, and the Em-

peror immediately ordered the Minister of War
to send supplies and aid to the commandant of
the frontiers, that all the border passes should
be watched, all mutiny suppressed, and that a
good General should be hurried off to the
locality.[1]

---

[1] These insurrections represent the normal state of things in
China. For many centuries this imperial authority has feebly maintained itself on the frontier provinces, and this Chapter may be
taken as a veritable fragment of every day history.

CHAPTER XLII.

YAO was removed from the War Administration and charged with the transport service
of the victualling department.

Knowing that his aunt had taken up her
abode in Tsien's palace, he went thither to pay
her his respects, and to bid her farewell.

When the Lady had admitted him, she wept
while he told her the purpose of his journey.

" The rebels have broken out into rebellion
on the frontiers, and a Han Lin doctor was dispatched in order to subdue them. That doctor
is my own nephew, Liang. But who could

10 *

have believed that his soldiers would be vanquished, and the rascally rebels triumph? It is sorrowful to think that such a youthful hero should have forsaken his parents, and have been thus sacrificed.

" By Imperial command, the Minister of War is sending stores and provisions, and I am ordered to accompany them. Therefore, have I come to bring my salutations,—to bid you farewell, not knowing whether I shall ever return."

The Lady, hearing this, burst into loud wailings: "The road to the frontiers is long and perilous. But when you reach the frontier you will write, and give us all the news about your uncle."

Having promised this, Yao departed,—but Yun Liang had overheard all the conversation.

CHAPTER XLIII.

SHE could scarcely contain her tears when she went to seek her mistress, and, with an agitation she could not control, she entered the boudoir.

She screamed out: " O my Lady! What a disaster—what a frightful disaster! It was on your account that Master Liang took the command of the troops. He has been slain on the battle field, and his soul is departed to the spiritland. Mr. Yao is gone to convey provisions to the troops, and has just been here to say farewell to our old lady. He related, in the saloon, what had happened to Master Liang. Your slave was present, and overheard it all!"

When Yao Sien heard this, it seemed as if life had departed from her,—there were streams of tears which indicated a broken heart. "It was for me that, careless of his own life,—for me, that he sacrificed himself. I will live no longer. I will not—cannot live alone. I will go to another world. I will join him there,—for he shall not be left to wander desolate on the earth. Alas! alas! that such a youth should have perished on my account. He is now a lonely and abandoned ghost." [1]

She loosened and shook her hair,—bent her head, over her ivory bed,—and poured out mournful lamentations. Never were there bitterer sobs,—never a more broken heart; at last, she sighed out:

"O Liang! wait for me in the yellow waters, till I can join you. I cannot remain in this wretched world. I would fain thank you for all your devotion to me, but here we can never be united,—never rest on the same pillow,—

---

[1] Wu Chu,—Without a master. If a person dies, leaving a son, the son becomes a *Chu*, (master) who directs all the funeral rites for his ancestors. If he have no son, he is Wu Chu, and no one is allowed to direct the services over the dead. The spirits of the childless dead are doomed to misery.

never repose under the same coverlet. Never
shall we sport in the garden together! Again
to see you is but a dream. I call upon you
with a thousand sobs, but there is no answer."

Exhausted and fainting, she fell upon her
bed, and, though she had been long weeping,
her tears flowed forth afresh.

But her body lost its strength, and her face
its beauty, and she was scarcely to be recognised. Night after night, hidden behind her
silken curtains, she pined away, from the dawn-
ing of the day to the departure of the evening.
As she refused all food,—even a handful of
rice,—or a drop of tea,—what wonder that her
lips were dry and her frame wasted!

Pi Yue, fearing that death would result from
the sufferings of her mistress, approached her
bedside, and said:

" Lady! arise, and take but a mouthful of
rice and tea! Do not make your parents
wretched on account of your truth and love.
If Liang have sacrificed himself for you, all
your grieving will not bring him back to life.
It is true, that the affection between lovers is
strong, but the heavenly goodness which our

parents have shown us, has a still stronger claim. Dear lady! Your mother bore you, and your father is in the midst of perplexities and difficulties; from which he is not returned. They expect you to perform for them the funeral rites, and that you will attend their departed spirits with the fragrant lamp.[1] If you give way because your lover is no more, on whom is your grey-headed father to depend? My old lady, too, has, for the last few days, had many griefs, and is mourning over her husband's absence. You must console her. You must not leave her to her sorrows, and break her heart, for your sickness will bring sickness to her, and make her very miserable."[2]

And thus, and in many other ways, did Pi Yue endeavour to comfort and to support her mistress.

Yao Sien sighed, and replied:

" Liang has died on my account, and the

---

[1] This is regarded as the highest of social duties, to which every other must be made subservient. Reverence for ancestors is of primary obligation, and its neglect is deemed infamous.

[2] Confucius insists on the necessity of filial obedience, on every occasion. He says: " In serving your parents, advise them with respectful gentleness,—observe and be attentive to all their wishes. Even if they deal harshly with you, do not murmur."

espoused husband has sacrificed himself to his espoused wife. If I do not preserve my faith and my chastity, how can I present myself to him in the yellow waters? I feel, indeed, all the goodness of my parents, but in spite of all, I cannot continue in this world. You tell me I must serve my mother when she is dead, and yet my parents insist on my betrothal. Now, if I obeyed them, and allowed them to betroth me, I shall have led my lover to a violent death. No! this can never be,—for I should for ever hate myself in the world below, while his bleached bones would remain on the battle-field. Though I must be disobedient, and refuse to be betrothed, I cannot tell my parents the true state of things. In whatever direction I turn, there is nothing but death before me, —and through the portals of death I shall rejoin my love."

Then, Yun Liang responded to the beautiful mourner:

"If this be the case, let us reconsider what is to be done! Master Liang has perished for your sake on the frontier, and you are determined that you will not be betrothed. Now, your father is besieged by the rebels, and we have no news of him: in his absence, the old lady will not venture to ask for the birth-certificates.[1]　When my Lord returns, the family will be all gathered together, and it will be a day of rejoicing, and if the marriage is spoken of, it will be a good time to discuss it."

Yao Sien turned over these councils in her heart.　She thought there was propriety in the suggestions of her maid.　" I really must do honour to my mother, and bear the burden of life, that I may serve her from morn to night. But I cannot forget the history of my lover. I will not forsake my betrothed, for that would break my heart.　Truly, my sorrow has no limit,—my tears no end.　All my life is linked to a heavy, heavy heart."

---

[1] A needful step towards marriage.　The record of birth is called *Sing King*.　It is accompanied with eight astrological signs, out of which the thaumaturgist reads the horoscope of the party, and decides whether, or not, the projected union is to be auspicious.

CHAPTER XLIV.

LIANG'S PARENTS HEAR OF THE DEATH OF
THEIR SON.

LEAVE we the young lady to her sorrows, and let us visit Liang's father and mother.

They had heard that their son's name had been placed on the golden list, with smiles, congratulations, and transports of joy.

One morning brought them a letter from their son, advising them that he had taken leave of the Emperor, and had gone to the borders to annihilate the accursed rebels. When the old gentleman had read it, his heart was sorrowful, and he said: " My son regards his life as of no more value than dust and dirt. The rebels, I know, are in great force on the frontier, and I do not believe that the ministers have taken any efficient measures for their subjugation, and for the protection of the public peace. I fear that my poor son will be sacrificed."

And this was the sole topic of conversation between the old people, from morn to night, and from day to day. But, on a certain day, when their brows were somewhat less furrowed with care, and their hearts somewhat lightened, there came undoubted information that their son was placed in the midst of difficulties and dangers. They smote their bosoms, and, in their distress, fell to the ground—

"O sorrow of sorrows! the youth is dead,— and none is left to bear the fragrant lamp to our funeral rites. Never shall our knees again feel the pressure of our son,—a son so noble and so virtuous,—who, in search of fame, has thrown his green youth away." They arose to mingle their tears, and it seemed as if they were to die together, and then each encouraged and consoled the other, read the sacred lessons, and made the needful preparations for the mourning. They clad themselves in funeral garments, set up the soul-plank, and poured out lamentations over their departed son.[1]

[1] On the death of relatives, the Chinese clothe themselves in coarse, unbleached garments, and exhibit an utter neglect of the toilet. They place a wooden plank, called *Ling Pai*, (soul-plank) on the altar table in the ancestral hall, upon which they display their offerings to the manes of the dead. The rites connected with reverence for ancestors, sometimes called "worship," are less of a religious, than a social character. They are practised alike by the Buddhists and Taoists, and by the free-thinkers, who call themselves followers of Confucius,—for it is an error to suppose that Confucius founded a religious sect, or ever assumed the authority of a religious teacher. The Jesuits, who settled in China nearly two centuries, rightly estimated the national character of the ancestral observances, and refused to denounce them as irreligious or unchristian; but when two of the Popes, misled by the representations of the more ignorant monks who had penetrated to Peking, instructed the Catholic missionaries to proclaim those observances as idolatrous and intolerable, the whole body of missionaries—many of whom, particularly those of the Society of Jesus, had obtained great influence at Court,—were expelled, and the fond hopes in which they had indulged, of Christianising the Chinese people, were scattered to the winds.

In the Institutes of the Chow dynasty, written for the promotion of "Peace and Tranquillity," about thirty centuries ago, the following passage is found: "The ancient kings honoured their forefathers and respected their ancestors, and accommodated their abundant offerings to the requirements of the great powers of heaven and earth. To heaven and earth the great sacrifices were made, and the noblest of all the sacrifices were made in the ancestral temple. Then followed the offerings to the gods of the land and grain, and then to the hundred spirits of the mountains and the rivers. There were sacrifices to the male, and others to the female principle of nature;

sacrifices to the celestial and terrestial divinities ; sacrifices to the ancient kings, and sacrifices to the manes of the dead."

A description of the funeral ceremonies, as now performed in the case of a person of rank, will be found in the Transactions of the N. China Branch of the Royal Asiatic Society, ii., 173—6. Here, the funeral procession passed through a door, denominated "Gate of the soul," beyond which, two wives, attired in mourning, with a white bandage round the forehead,—their cheeks being painted with fictitious tears, stood before a picture. A herald of the dead, called "Opening road spirit," preceded the rest, and the multitudes that followed, which scattered, lavishly, paper representing Sycee silver, which is believed to conciliate the malignity of evil spirits by seeming to recompense, and then disappointing their cupidity. The chair of the deceased, hidden under a veil, lest he should witness the grief of his friends left in this world, and a mourning lantern, to enable him to recognise the friends whom he would meet in another, were among the many characteristic insignia of the ceremonial.

The place selected for burial is an object of great solicitude, and among the opulent, the coffins (often very costly and highly adorned) are frequently kept for many years, to afford time for the choice of a spot which will be grateful to the departed spirit. Tombs are generally built by rich people in the shape of a horse shoe, in whose centre, it is believed the disembodied ghost is wont, unseen, to sit, and to enjoy the beautiful scenery around. Necromancers are employed to examine the soil, and to report on the landscape. Howqua, the great Hong merchant, told me that his father had been dead many years, and that he had not yet determined on the place for his burial. In the great cities, there are temporary receptacles for coffins. I have seen hundreds piled upon one another,—where they were kept above ground, waiting for their final disposal.

CHAPTER XLV.

YU KHING THINKS ABOUT HER PERSONAL HONOUR.

THE news of Liang's death reached the palace of the Minister, and sadly affected Liu. He and his wife reported the event to their daughter. She burst into tears: " So talented a youth— sacrificed on the border. Who shall gather together his bones,—who shall bring his body to the graves of his ancestors?"[1]

She said no more, but repaired to her chamber, and took out her silk garments.

---

[1] So great is the desire to be buried near the tombs of their forefathers, that vessels are sometimes freighted from Australia and California, to convey to the family graves, for interment, the coffins which contain the remains of those who have died in exile.

"Never, from this day forth, will I wear a silk garment again! I will adorn myself no longer. I will never wear a flower. Nature has no charms for me. I will bid farewell to the garden. I will give myself to solitude, that I may think only of my lost lord."

And so she rouged herself no longer,—she dropped her paint-box, and was sorely afflicted.

When her chamber-maid saw the grief of her mistress, and how she was bewailing him who was betrothed to her, she endeavoured to comfort her.

"May I ask, now, why you are so woe-begone, and why fall these floods of tears? I have heard something of your engagement with Liang, but there is no reason for this excess of sorrow. For though you were betrothed, you have never met him, and the projected alliance is but a dead letter. Many are the betrothals of those who may have loved in a former world, but they have broken by death, and the betrothed, after seven weeks[1] of mourning, have talked of new betrothals, and before the ground is dry,[2] another marriage is settled.

[1] The appointed time for mourning is seven times seven days.
[2] Sir John Davis, in his China and the Chinese, refers to the tra-

" How many quarrels there are in the world.

dition, which Voltaire has also popularised in his " Zadig," and
which explains what is meant by " drying the ground." Chwang
Tze, one of the disciples of the famous Lao Tze, the founder of the
Taoist sect, was taking his country walks, and at the foot of a mountain he came to a number of graves.   He had been musing upon
death, which makes its victims equally among rich and poor, when
he saw a grave, over which a young lady, in mourning garments, was
bending, holding a white fan in her hand, with which she diligently
fanned the grave.   Chwang Tze inquired the meaning of this singular
proceeding, but the lady gave him no answer, except by bursting into
tears, which the philosopher regarded as evidence that modesty had
closed her lips.   At last, however, she said : " I am a widow, and this
is my husband's grave, who very lately died. He was very fond of me,
and said to me, on his death-bed, ' Beloved wife ! if you ever think
of a second marriage, consent, at least, to wait till my grave is dry.'
Now, as I have discovered that fresh earth is not speedily dried, I
have taken to fanning it, that it may dry the sooner."   The philosopher then took the white fan, and, with a stroke of magic, dried
up the ground.   The widow warmly expressed her gratitude, and
desired he would accept the white fan as a memento of his friendly
services.   But the tradition is carried farther in the Chinese records.
Chwang Tze is said to have reported the matter to his wife, who expressed great indignation against the widow ; but Chwang having died
soon after, his widow became enamoured of one of his disciples, who,
when seized with a violent cholic, was advised that a human molar
tooth was the best remedy ; hearing which, she opened her late husband's coffin, and endeavouring to extract the tooth, he was roused by
the pain.   She fled, and hanged herself for shame.   Chwang Tze made
a drum out of a tub, and went about telling the story.   In his travels, he reached the eastern river, where some small fishes, on the
bank which was almost dry, said to him : " If you can bring the
western to join the eastern river, you will save us from the death
with which we are threatened."   Chwang listened to their petition
and the fishes were saved.   He was visited by a dream that he had
been transformed into a butterfly,—his true existence,—for that being
a butterfly before, he had dreamed he was a man.

A man may prefer his first to his second wife,—and a woman her first, to her second husband. And who takes any notice of this? All girls are willing to consent to a second betrothal when the first has failed. Why should you care about a man whose face you have never seen? No doubt he was an excellent youth, who, in early life, had obtained distinction, and on whose memory you may dwell with pleasure."

Yu Khing could not check a deep sigh, and she thus replied to her chamber-maid:

"Hold! for you sorely afflict me. Modesty has every where its praise, but levity and profligacy tear up the social relations.[1] In ancient days, some flung themselves into an abyss,[2]— some cut off their hand,[3] in proof of their affec-

---

[1] The social relations of the first order are those betweeen sovereign and subject (1), father and son (2), husband and wife (3).

[2] The daughter of Fung, of Fo Hae, was married to the book-censor, Tin. They both fell into the hands of bandits, and, on their endeavouring to escape, Tin died of grief, and three of her female slaves, in order to show their affection for their mistress, took the hand of each, and destroyed themselves by leaping into a deep pit.

[3] Wang Ying was an official who was charged with taking the census of the population in the district of Kue. He died while engaged in his duty. His family was poor, and his only descendant a little boy. His wife, whose maiden name was Li, came with her son

tion, and in reverence for the five primal virtues,[1] and their fame has come down to our
time. Seiu Mei had never seen the face of
her husband, but she condemned herself to
perpetual widowhood.[2]

"I care nothing for luxury and display.   I

and the bones of her husband, to an inn at Khai Fung. When the
landlord saw that she had only her son as a companion, he mistrusted
her, and would not give her a night's lodging. Li, seeing that it grew
dark, refused to go, so he took her by the arm and turned her out of
the door. She turned her eyes to heaven, wept bitterly, and said :
" I am but a poor woman, and cannot defend my own honour. He has
seized me by the hand, but he shall not, on that account, pollute my
whole body. So she took a hatchet and severed her arm from her
body. When the passengers saw this, they admired the virtue of Li,
and the magistrate of Khai Fung, hearing of the adventure, told it
to the Emperor. He also gave her medicine to heal the wound, and
lent her other assistance. The landlord was severely bastinadoed.

[1] The five primal virtues are (1) benevolence, (2) rectitude
(3) propriety, (4) wisdom, and (5) truthfulness. References, as in
this case, to aphorisms and traditions are considered evidences of
cultivation, and are highly appreciated in conversation. I have often
known an argument at once brought to a close by a fictitious reference to the words of a sage, or the records of an annalist.

[2] Sieu Mei was betrothed to Chang Liu. He fell sick. Sieu Mei
sent her female slave, Ngai Yu, to inquire about him. Chang Lin
dallied with Ngai Yu, and died in consequence. When Sieu Mei
heard of the death of Chang Liu, she made a vow that she would
never marry again, which she kept faithfully,—remaining a virgin to
the end of her days. But her slave bore a son, who was named after
his father, Chang Liu. Afterwards, the boy became a very learned
man, and was promoted to a high literary grade, in the time of the
Ming dynasty.

11

would willingly live in a small hut, to obtain, in the after world, reputation for a thousand or ten thousand years. But as I cannot be a heroine among men, I will not marry again, for I have no desire to be the mock of the market-place, or the scorn of the street rabble, to whom chastity is valueless as dust. Some there are, careless about such matters, and who prefer wedding to widowhood, and care not if their lovers perish, provided they can marry again. But do they not know that it is the will of God which directs the concerns of men, and that they may get nothing better than a poor wretch for a husband. And with what face can such people look upon the world, and with what face will the world look upon them? I will not marry upon earth, but leave revelry and delight and sensuality to those who can enjoy them. Only let my parents take charge of my chaste reputation, and I will hide myself behind my curtain in peace, and render them all becoming service. But if they will not allow to be ruled by my own heart and my own wishes, I will mount the white, wandering, lonely clouds."[1]

---

[1] I will destroy myself.

Her chamber and serving maids offered her their earnest condolence. " Lady! indeed we mourn that you are wasting your green spring. There are not many girls in the world so beautiful as you, and you cannot always be the guardian of your own modesty. You must not waste your lovely years,—you must not destroy your life's felicity, and if here you bear no dishonoured name, little matters it when you are dead, if you are talked of or not."

Yu Khing was irritated at such language: " Your counsel is despicable. Can a sparrow understand the heart of a swan? Will a phœnix join the wild hens? When the mandarin duck loses her mate, she pairs not again,—and if a goose wander away from her flock, she will remain a solitary creature. Now, if birds and beasts preserve their faith and their purity, shall not we do so, who, from our youth upwards, have been taught the lessons of propriety? Your words may be attractive as

---

[1] Many are the councils and the traditions which represent second marriages as unbecoming. A sage, when asked whether a poverty-struck widow might not marry a second husband, answered : " Cold and hunger may excuse much,—but starvation is better than disgrace."

flowered silk, but that will not prevent the streaming waters from carrying away the fallen leaves."

The maidens dared not answer, and Yu Khing was left to her own melancholy reflections.

Another tradition says : "A princess, having lost her husband, told her father that she wished to be married again. 'And whom would you like to marry?' he enquired,—and she answered: 'The minister, Lung.' The Emperor having proposed the exalted match, Lung replied: 'It is impossible,—my wife and I have suffered poverty together. I cannot degrade her to be my concubine, and my concubine the princess cannot be.'"

In the life of Confucius, it is related that, he found, in his walks, a widow, weeping bitterly over a grave. He said: "You must have had many sorrows,—your tears are so many." "Many, indeed," she replied: "That a tiger had killed her brother,—another, her husband,—and a third her son." "Why do you not marry again?" enquired the sage. And the widow answered: "I dare not violate the law." "You say well!" was the reponse of Confucius. "Violators of the law," has become the ordinary term of reprobation for bad Mandarins.

CHAPTER XLVI.

A REMEDY PRESENTS ITSELF TO LIANG.

WHILE the pretty maiden was thus engaged with her perplexities, Liang had still greater perplexities and troubles. He was beleaguered in the mountains without any opening for escape. He had only a few thousand soldiers to resist the numerous cavalry and infantry of the rebels. Happily, the mountain streams furnished abundant supplies of water, and as provisions were not wanting, neither hunger nor thirst were feared. But, as the relief-troops did not appear, Liang was more discouraged day by day. So he summoned together his staff and officers, and said to them:

" Listen to me while I speak frankly to you.
It is useless that you should share my fate, and
I, cannot conceal from you that I see no pros-
pect of saving my own life. You may take
advantage of my position, and come to terms
by delivering me over to the enemy. You
will thus save your own lives, and I will readily
surrender myself to die."

The soldiers were greatly moved, and answered : " General! Why will you not rely on
on us? Your goodness has treated us like
brothers, and shall we, for that goodness, make
an ungrateful return? We have ample provisions for a month, and we will hold out in
expectation of relief, and if it fail us, we will,
with all our strength, force our way through
the mountain passes. Life and death hang
upon fate, but you shall find us loyal and faithful, determined to merit the favour of the
Imperial Ruler."

Hearing this, the spirit of Liang revived.
He determined that there should be no surrender, and directed that the outposts should
be carefully watched.

When the rebels saw what precautions he

had taken, they decided not to attack him. They said his provisions would soon be exhausted, and he would be forced to deliver himself into their hands. He was a bird in a cage, and even had he wings to fly, it was impossible he should escape.

CHAPTER XLVII.

LIU PRESSES HIS DAUGHTER TO MARRY.

LET us come down from the mountains to visit
Lady Liu. She said to herself: " Liang is
dead, and, from the earliest times, maidens
have been encouraged by their parents to
marry." So she ordered the birth-certificate
of her daughter to be prepared, and looked
round in search of a becoming son-in-law.
She sent back all the presents she had received
from Liang's family. In the district, there
dwelt a young man, the son of a functionary,
called Lan. Lan was employed in the public
service, and was a man of considerable opulence. He had heard of the talents and beauty

of the young Lady Liu, and engaged a match-
maker to go to the house of her father.

Having obtained access to the presence of
the old Lady Liu, he knelt down at her feet,
and thus addressed her:

" My Lady Lan sends you her hearty salutations, and asks your young daughter in marriage for her third son. He is a most agreeable young gentleman, and is just entering
his nineteenth year. He is the ablest student
in Su Chow, and comes out first in every
examination. His family has a mountain of
gems and treasures, and, in addition, is a very
handsome fellow,—indeed, the handsomest fellow in the world."

The old lady was delighted with the pro-
posal, and hurried into the saloon to communicate it to her husband. He answered: " Is not
our daughter already engaged? You know
her obstinacy, and I do not believe she will
listen to you."

And, having said this, he rose up and went
out of the door. My Lady then sent for her
daughter, and spoke of the offer,—that it would
be for her happiness to secure so desirable a

11 *

husband. The young lady threw herself at her mother's feet,—pearly tears fell down her cheeks, while she said: "No! no! I am betrothed to Mr. Liang, and to him my person belongs. This talent-full youth has been sacrificed on the frontiers, and his solitary ghost is wandering about to my deep sorrow. His heart and body are not yet cold, and you come to talk to me of another marriage. How should I ever escape the upbraidings of Liang's family! From of old, the swallow that has lost her mate wanders about disconsolate, and will not pair again. And shall I, a chaste maiden, think of espousing a second husband? Neither let you nor my father be anxious about me, who only desire to sleep in a lonely bed for what remains of life. I will serve you as I ought,—and like a waning moon, or a fading flower, pass into old age."[1]

But the old Lady Liu severely reprimanded

[1] As a full moon and a fully developed fragrant flower are deemed the representatives of fortunate and responsive love,—so the moon in its decline, and the flowers, when withered, betoken unrequited and disappointed affection. This poetical phraseology enters into the ordinary conversation of the Chinese, especially the more cultivated classes.

her daughter. "Why should you profess an attachment to this young man, whom you have not known,—never seen, and have never stretched the scarlet thread to one another?[1] Such a marriage was never predestined, never registered in heaven. He is dead, and is no more to you than any stranger you may meet in your walks. But I have sought for you a charming young man,—altogether worthy and distinguished,—him you shall possess, and be happy to the end of your existence."

Yu Khing responded, with a sigh: "Beloved mother mine! You speak thoughtlessly. You say that Liang is a stranger,—but I am betrothed to him for life. And though we have not personally interchanged our domestic pledges, my honour and word shall be faithfully kept."[2]

Here the match-maker interposed, and said: "You are entangled by false notions of love. Is it not said,—and has it not been said from

[1] When betrothals take place, the bridegroom and bride drink out of cups which are linked to one another with a scarlet thread. Matrimony is therefore allegorically called "The red thread" or "scarlet filament."

[2] Original.—My word is worth a thousand pieces of gold.

the oldest time,—that marriage is a mandate of heaven, and that a lovely girl belongs to an accomplished youth?[1] The first thing is to obtain the birth certificate. But you must let me tell you something about the opulence of young Lan. He is of a most distinguished family, and if you do not accept him, you will commit a terrible mistake. That his father is an official of high rank, I need not repeat to you. The Son of heaven is one of his sworn friends.[2] Amber and coral are but sweepings for him,—pearls and precious stones are but sand and dirt. The park is magnificent; with willows on the left, and flowers on the right-hand side. He has a hundred beautiful female slaves, clothed in heavy satin, and, in summer, in gauze silk.

"If you like chess, you will be among chess proficients. You will play upon the guitar, and there will be a harp always at your dis-

---

[1] Literally, that "a rosy cheek belongs to a green jade-stone." Jade is reckoned among the precious stones in China,—that of a light green colour is most appreciated.

[2] The commentator says: "Here the matchmaker exhibits extraordinary effrontery to deal so daringly with the Imperial name." It was, however, in the way of business.

posal. There is a charming terrace, where you may listen to jasper flutes, with lute accompaniments. Even the serving maidens are delighted with their position, and how much more delighted will the mistress of the serving maidens be! The young gentleman is clever and handsome,—nothing of a scapegrace. He is very intelligent, very virtuous, and of a noble house. He has passed through the first and second literary grades, and the hand-writing of his examination papers is beautiful as flowery silk, or silken flowers.[1] He is benevolent, modest, and from all festivities returns directly home.[2]

" He is thoroughly acquainted with all the proprieties, knows all the becoming salutations, and how to direct the female slaves to set fine tea before his guests. Idle fellows are proud, and carry their eyes aloft,—that is but an old

[1] Beautiful hand-writing is the first step to literary eminence in China.—Note to p. 194.

[2] Those who have occasion to become acquainted with the profligacy of Chinese youths, in connection with these festivals, and the habits of adjournment from the outpourings at the table, to other scenes of revelry and licentiousness, will understand the compliment conveyed in the matchmaker's eulogium.

saying,—but his face, in the presence of every-body, is as sweet as a flower. If you marry him, be assured you will do better than if you entered the Imperial palace. Come,—do not be so silly as to talk of widowhood. You are preparing for your heart all the perplexities of tangled flax. Youth cannot subdue the im-pulses of the affections, and self-reproach and shame will follow our own blunders."

When Yu Khing heard this, she was inwardly exasperated. "Mistress Lang! trouble us not with such cxaggerated talk. You say that, because I am young, I cannot remain a widow, but I have not the slightest intention to take up my lute, and to enter into any other family. And however good Mr. Lan may be, I will not have him. Give yourself no farther trouble with your silk embroidery. I know the arts of your profession, and that, of ten words you utter, nine are false."

The old lady here commanded the beautiful girl to be silent: "Hold your tongue, daughter. Your father has to be consulted. It is for your parents to do what is proper."

Saying, this, her face grew gloomy, and she said stealthily to the matchmaker: "This affair must be left to my management. Let no one talk about it."

Mrs. Wang returned home,—and Yu Khing, weeping, entered her own apartments.

CHAPTER XLVIII.

YU KHING FLINGS HERSELF INTO THE RIVER.

WHEN she had entered her bed-room, she loosened her adorned hair, flung herself upon her ivory bed, and exclaimed: " Sorrow upon sorrow! That I should be so overwhelmed with affliction! This very evening I will depart. I will fling myself into the river of death, and tell my lover, in the other world, all that has happened to me in this."

And then she heard the birds returning with the descent of evening, and the rooks were cawing on the branches of the trees.

" Now is the time when I must seek for death, for I have no hope of finding peace or brightness in life." And she broke out into loud lamentations.

"Why should I live merely to marry an opulent man? Must I leave my mother,—must I forsake my father,—and end my wretched existence? If I, with a knife, cut the cord of life, my body will remain, and cause grief to my parents. I had better fling myself into the river. Sorrow of sorrows! that I should die so young,—die without a chance of coming back to earth. But I must abandon this world, and seek the yellow waters of my lover's grave. I can only thus relieve my overflowing heart. O bitter thought, that I should perish in the watery wave!"

She set her various belongings in order, and clothed herself in her best garments. Bathed in tears, she uttered, in her inmost thoughts, farewell to her parents. "I am making an ungrateful return to my mother, for her kindness in bringing me up. There is no hope for her ever to see her daughter again,—my brothers must take charge of the house. I shall be whelmed in the waters. So only can my honour be preserved."

Having said this, she left her bed-room, and entered the front apartment. Her golden lilies stamped the floor,—she smote her breast, and addressed her prayers to heaven. Tears flooded her cheeks, and she uttered lamentations over her unhappiness,—to die so young—so young and so unfortunate. "Am I not to be pitied, thus driven to seek the yellow waters? Never again shall I see my jewels,—never again look upon my toilet casket. Hope has abandoned me,—pleasure is departed for ever. But to-night shall see the triumph of faithful love between man and wife. The moon is waning, —the flowers are fading,—my youth is destroyed. But rather than be betrothed, I will throw myself into the river, and save my honour from shame."

She opened the door of the back garden, and entered hastily in. She looked up, and saw the bright moon illuminating the circle of the heavens. "The moon is at its full, but human sorrows are not healed. My sorrows, indeed, are entitled to sympathy. This day twelve-month will be kept as the anniversary of my death,—for, on this night of this year, the river

will overwhelm me. It is sad to think that all the
cares and all the kindness I have received from
my parents, during eighteen years, should end
in nothingness."

She hurried towards the banks of the river,
and looked upon the broad water streaming
towards the east. Two tear drops—and two
more tear drops dimmed her eyes.

"The deep waters of the river will be the goal
of my life, and I withdraw my hand from all
the foulness of the world. I am like a pure
and precious flower, blasted by the storm and
swept away by the rain. The blossoms do not
last long,—the leaves are driven about by the
whirlwind, and carried off by the fleeting waters.
'Tis human destiny, and will be repeated from
year to year,—but when I am departed, shall
I return again?"

She raised her head—looked up—and saw
the moon fixed in the heavens. "O moon!
thou shinest on a maiden among women, who,
in order to avoid second espousals with Lan,
forsakes her mother, abandons her father, and
has now approached the banks of the river, and
following the example of Tsien, will fling herself

into the stream.[1] It is because I will remain a widow, and refuse obedience to my mother, who insists on my marrying again, that I abandon life in its young spring, and will not wait for the coming of the autumnal season. And when I have given my body to the river, in the boundless waters I shall find repose. Goddess of the moon! I supplicate thy aid. Let me not fall into the shallows, but into the depths of the stream."

This, saying, she threw herself into the water. Who would have dreamed that a boat man was at hand to hear her lamentations, and prevent the accomplishment of her heart's desire?

[1] Tsien Yu Lien was the wife of Wang Chi Phang, a Mandarin in the service of the Emperor Kao Tsung, of the Jung dynasty, (A. D. 1127—62.)

Wang was sent, by the Emperor, against the Kin Tartars, who, by stratagem, had captured two of the former Emperors of China, Hwui Tsing and Kin Tsong. A certain Sun Iu Khiun, who desired to possess the person of Tsien Yu Lien, endeavoured to seduce her husband's step-mother to sell her to him. For this purpose, he procured a falsified document, by which Wang divorced his wife, which bore the forged signature of Wang. On hearing that she had been divorced by her husband, Tsien Yu flung herself into the river and was drowned. Wang returned, and brought funereal offerings to the banks of the river. This is one of many stories in a large collection of biographies, entitled *King Chai Ki*,—"History of unfortunate women."

CHAPTER XLIX.

A PROVINCIAL EXAMINER SAVES, AND INTER-
ROGATES HER.

BUT so it was. The boat of a provincial examiner, named Lung, in which he was living with his family, was anchored on the bank of the river.[1] Two lazy steermen had charge of the boat. They had heard cries of distress,

---

[1] These family boats are found on all the canals and rivers of China. They are fitted up with every domestic convenience,—have frequently a suite of apartments, and are, in fact, ambulatory houses, in which long journeys are made, for purposes of business or plea- sure. I have been struck with the many accommodations provided, and know of no more agreeable way of visiting and tarrying at regions, most of whose attractions are on, or adjacent to, the shores of rivers or canals. The principal impediments are the shallows,— the currents,—or the weirs (Pah), over which it is needful to get assistance to drag the boats.

but waited for orders, and took no steps to save Yu Khing.[1] She was in the water, and was carried rapidly away towards the east. But the examiner ordered the boatmen to spring into the water and to save the lovely maiden.[2] The master obeyed the examiner's commands, and, after many efforts, succeeded in rescuing Yu Khing, and brought her in safety to the boat. Lung and his wife eagerly enquired into the motives which had induced her to commit so dreadful a deed? " Everybody fears death, and what can have induced you to abandon life, and to fling yourself into the eastward rushing water?"

Yu Khing answered, weeping : " It was caused by a thousand sorrows. I have been educated in an honourable house, and belong

[1] This is characteristic of the Chinese. I have known robberies take place in crowded streets, with not the slightest interference from passengers, or from persons looking out of their doors and windows, while the offences were committed. People were constantly drowned in Hong Kong, in the presence of those who might have saved them without any peril to themselves, and I was obliged to issue an ordinance, condemning the boats to confiscation, whose owners refused to rescue those who had fallen into the water.

[2] This, again, is a trait of Chinese manners. Boatmen would not dare disobey the orders of a literary Mandarin invested with authority.

to a distinguished family.[1]   My father is a Minister, and his name is Liu.   I have not been wanting in any of the proprieties, have discharged every womanly duty, and have passed a quiet and spotless life.[2]

" I was betrothed to a son of Mr. Liang's family.   He, in search of honour, went to the Imperial Court, and there having obtained the highest rank in literary distinction, was nominated to the Han Lin College.   He entered upon an engagement to attack the rebels, in order to obtain the approval of the Supreme Ruler. But, unexpectedly, his life was sacrificed on the frontiers.   My parents urged upon me another pairing of the phœnixes.[3]   They represented to me that it was not becoming I should remain a virgin,—that I ought to accept another husband,—again to braid my hair, shave my eyebrows,[4] and embark on another nuptial voyage.

---

[1] The demarcations between different ranks in China, though they have not the character of " Caste," are seen in all the social relations, and are provided for, not only by official and Imperial orders, but are recognised in the classical books of antiquity.

[2] I was brought up in maidenly privacy,—taught all the duties of womanhood, and lived a tranquil and a happy life.

[3] To consent to a second auspicious marriage.

[4] Chinese ladies shave the hair from their eye-brows, and paint the

" But I was not willing to consent to another betrothal, and I supplicated my parents in vain that they should not insist on carrying out their purpose. And I thought that, if, for the preservation of life, I sacrificed my honour, an infamy would attach to my name, which no time would ever remove. And death is inevitable,—it will come at last, though we should live a hundred years. Die we all must, but I would die with the reputation of chastity, and leave an honourable memory behind me. So I quitted the home of my fathers, and flung myself into the river, that my sorrows might be drowned in the swift-flowing waters."

When Lady Lin heard this, she pitied her sincerely: " And so you wished to shorten your lovely years,—and it was to save your chaste reputation. Really, you must be the most virtuous woman within the four seas." [1]

And the old gentleman responded to the beautiful maiden: " Unbosom your heart to

spot with a regular arch, so as to give prominence and regularity to the features. As men, in the time of mourning, neglect their beards, so women allow the growth of their hair as evidence of grief.

[1] " The four seas," which, according to ancient Chinese geography form the boundaries of the world.

us, and mourn no longer. And you really flung yourself into the river to save your name and fame? But I shall convey you home, and you shall enjoy not only the spring, but the autumn of life, and the society of mankind. And I shall counsel your parents to submit to your wishes. You shall remain pure and happy behind your curtains, and you shall be spared from future vexations."

Yu Khing answered, checking the tears which had been dropping: "Lady! listen to my words. Had my parents been willing to comply with my wishes, I had certainly not flung myself into the river. But though they now consent that I may remain a widow, after two or three autumns, they will insist on finding me a husband. And then my vows will be broken and my honour be wounded. I will not live a life of wretchedness. The pencil shall erase my name from the mortal calendar.[1] My hope and prayer is that you

[1] Yen Wang, one of the kings or judges of hell, is, according to the Buddhist creed, the registrar of the birth of every human being, and when the doom of death is pronounced against any mortal, the pencil of Yen obliterates his name from the list,—and he is supposed to pass to the tribunal of judgment, where his merits and demer⁴⁺·

will leave me to my fate, and allow me to be carried away by the deep, driving stream. I would that my poor body should be the prey of the fishes of the river. I was born to an unhappy destiny, and it cannot be altered now."

The good old lady answered: " Think not so meanly of your body, and desire not to visit the world below. I am sixty years old. I have never been blessed with children, and, after my death, I shall be blown about like a tempest-driven cloud.[1] I see that you are a virtuous maiden, and my heart feels an affection for you. I will adopt you from this very day as my daughter. You shall remain with me as long as I live, and I will console you in all your sorrows. You may serve us as long as you live, and when we die, you shall be free, you may cut off your hair and become a nun."[2]

will be weighed against one another, and a higher or a lower destiny awarded in the next stage of existence, according to the preponderance of his virtues or vices.

[1] No greater misery than to be childless,—that the departed spirit should not be tranquillized by the performance of the furreral rites, for which it is the primary duty of the descendants of the departed to provide. Until performed, the spirit is a restless, houseless wanderer, "a tempest driven cloud."

[2] I once entered a Nunnery, in China. The general regulations resemble those of the less severe orders of the Catholic Sisterhoods.

The old gentleman concurred with this: "Yes! you shall remain with us, and we will make our mutual lives comfortable."

Yu Khing gratefully knelt down: "Lady! your goodness and virtue are larger than a mountain."

They ordered dry clothes to be brought. Their tenderness was that of a mother to a child, and Yu Khing was consoled. She became calm and resigned. At the break of the following day, the anchor was raised, and the boat continued on its voyage.

The appearance of the nuns resembles that of the Buddhist priests' who have, also, their heads shorn, and are clothed in coarse, yellow garments.

CHAPTER L.

YU KHING'S PARENTS HEAR OF THE CATASTROPHE,
AND GO FORTH TO SEEK THE BODY.

AND now that Yu Khing is saved, we will speak again of the old minister, Lin. He had risen early in the morning, and was sitting with his wife, when the servants rushed in, crying out: "We know not what is become of the young lady. All her belongings are packed up in her bed-chamber,—every door is open,— and no trace of her is to be found."

When the mother heard this, she screamed, stamped with her feet, and beat her breast, exclaiming: "Where is my daughter?" She directed everybody to go forth in search,—but they returned one after another, all declaring they had no news to give. She was no where to be found. They had enquired of everybody, and could learn nothing; but one of them had seen a boatman on the river, who reported that he had heard, in the previous evening, sighs and groans,—that, afterwards, there was a splash in the water, of which he had thought nothing, as he supposed some one had plunged in to bathe.[1] The old man became very angry, and flung reproaches at his wife: "Short-sighted woman! You knew that our daughter would not consent, and instead of treating her with gentleness and kindness,—instead of condoling with, and comforting her, you drove her to despair, and she has flung herself into the ocean.[2] You could not have loved—you must have hated your daughter."

Saying this, he ordered the whole household to seek for his daughter's body in the river.

The mother was overwhelmed with grief.

[1] It has been before remarked that, indifference to the sufferings of others, and unwillingness to take any trouble to aid or save a fellow creature, are Chinese idiosyncracies. It is sometimes worse than this. I have seen a corpse remaining for hours under the table of gamblers; and little children, as well as their parents, laughing over victims of any painful accident.

[2] River, sea, and ocean, are used sometimes synonymously by the Chinese.

CHAPTER LI.

THE ARROW STRATAGEM.

WE shall not tarry now to accompany Lin in the search of his daughter, but accompany the relief troops and transports, which were sent from the capital to the frontier. Their arrival was immediately reported to the General Commandant. He heard that Liang had not been captured or destroyed, but for more than a month had been beleaguered in the mountains by the rebels. As soon as Yao was informed of this, he hurried to the head quarters of the General, in the camp, and asked leave to take the command of a select body of the soldiery, and to conduct them to the battle-field. The

General perceived that the youth was bold and adventurous, and complied with his request, allowing him to pick out fifty thousand of the most courageous of the troops, who were placed under his command. Upon which, Yao left the camp, in order to mature his plans.

"These impious rebels are so strong, that no one has dared to attack them. My brother Liang has been long besieged by them, yet if we can concert our schemes together, we shall not fail of success; but if he act alone, he will be surprised and overthrown."

He ordered no movement against the enemy among the troops whom he had gathered together, but went out secretly in the moonlight to reconnoitre for himself. He remained absent from the camp more than half a night, which he passed clambering among the mountains, that he might make a complete survey. He saw that the rebels were scattered about in a very disorderly manner, and were principally encamped at the foot of a hill, but there was, obviously, little discipline among them, and the different corps were far away from one another. Yao's spirit rejoiced when he discovered the state of things: "They can know nothing of my arrival. A single valorous soldier might scatter them. Ere long, I shall rescue my brother Liang."

He returned to the camp, and wrote two letters, and taking with him two whistling arrows,[1] he again sought the top of the mountain. He knelt down reverently, and poured out this prayer to the spirits of the four quarters: "I have devoted myself to the service of the empire and the Emperor. I am willing to sacrifice my life if I can disperse the rebels. Thus, first, as a servant of the State I shall do my duty; secondly, my devotion will be made known to the world; thirdly, I shall save my uncle; and fourthly, I shall deliver my brother. I am willing to mingle with the dust, but I supplicate the sublimity of heaven to grant my suppliant prayer."

The two letters were to announce his arrival. He attached a letter to each of the whistling arrows, and shot the first into the border city. It was addressed to his uncle, Major-General

[1] Arrows, to which a musical pipe is attached, and when launched, they make a loud whizzing, or whistling in the air.

Yang, and invited him to a conference for the following evening, during the second watch,[1]— in order to arrange for an attack upon the enemy. He requested an immediate answer for his guidance.

The second arrow he shot to the camp of his brother on the hills, to inform him of what was doing.

[1] 9—11, P. M.

CHAPTER LII.

THE VICTORY IS WON AND THEY RETURN TO COURT.

WE shall not now record what were Yao's plans for the salvation of the State, but visit Liang as he was surrounded by the rebels. A month had passed,—his resources were almost exhausted, and all his troops were dejected and disconsolate,—given over to mourning and lamentation. At the sounding of the fourth drum, he went to the mountain top, to make his observations, and to meditate on any plans for success. Suddenly, he heard the whistle of a dispatch-arrow passing over his head,—it fell on the side of the mountain, and stuck in the grass sod. Liang hastened to pick it up, and found a letter attached to the arrow. He hurriedly opened it, and was overwhelmed with transports of joy. With a smothered voice, he called his officers together, and communicated to them the glad tidings that Yao was coming for their deliverance. " He has written to me that, to-morrow evening, at the second watch, there will be a signal of a musket shot, on hearing which, we are to sally forth to meet the Imperial flag."

And he dispatched an answer to Yao, informing him that his letter had been received.

The unexpected news was so welcome to the troops, that their spirits revived, and they were eager for the combat. All day they were on the watch, until the fall of evening. And Liang thus addressed the soldiery: " Victory or defeat depends upon yourselves. Now is the time for action. Despise death, and you will save your lives."

His words filled the hearts of his troops with enthusiasm. The signal shot was heard, —the flash was seen in the air. Yao's troops came out from their encampment, and separated into two divisions. One marched upon the city, and broke through the advanced guard of the enemy; the other defiled towards the mountain on the farther side. The rebels, in their unconcern and self-confidence, had been given up to drunken revelries, and as they found themselves on all sides surrounded by Chinese soldiers, they were distressed that they could find no wings to take flight through the air. Regardless of danger and death, the Chinese fought, and every one of them was worth a hundred men, and pressed forward on every side, overwhelming all resistance. They were brave and active, full of zeal and fire, and they destroyed the accursed rebels as if they were cutting clay. Five hundred thousand rebels[1] were slaughtered before the break of day, and the blood that streamed down from the mountains formed a lake below. Having

[1] Extravagant and hyperbolical forms of expression characterise most of the literature. There is a simple word *I*, for "Stop," yet the common phrase is,—"Ten thousand times there is no stoppage." The word *wan*, meaning "ten thousand," is habitually used to represent any great number of objects. The Chinese are particularly reckless and untrustworthy where figures are concerned, · not always, perhaps, attributable to a purpose of mendacity,—but partly to carelessnes of observation, and, still more, to the general employment of a magniloquent phraseology.

thus extinguished the enemy, the Chinese soldiers broke up the camp, gathered themselves together, and cooked their rice, in order to slake their hunger.

Liang, Yao, and the Major-General met, in order to hold a council of war. "We must now turn this slaughtering of the accursed rebels to account, and destroy all their hiding places, before we lead our troops away." They all agreed in opinion, and decided to break up the camp, to put the troops in motion, and to gather together the standards and the flags. All the wounded rebels surrendered at discretion, and submitted to authority. So, were the rebels dispersed, for the trio of Generals were expert in all the arts of war; and some other rebel officers, hearing the results of the fray, presented themselves, and lowered their flags to the conquerors. The rebel city was utterly destroyed, and the ring-leaders were all made prisoners.[1] Miserable was the woe,

---

[1] This is a very fair specimen of ordinary Chinese exaggeration. Abundance of descriptions of battles, like this narrative, will be found, to this day, in tho Peking Gazettes, describing the manner in which the rebels have been routed. I once witnessed a battle between the Imperial troops and the insurgents. They abused one another

and many the tears, of the captured. They were packed up in the prison cages,[1]—while the army returned, singing songs of victory.

from a distance,—each challenged their opponents to "come forward,"—called them "scoundrels and cowards,"—the ranks broke up,—and the combat became a fight of man to man. They advanced, —retreated—advanced again—fired, and ran away ; very few were wounded, and fewer killed ; but when the hour for eating came,— both parties left the field "to cook their rice." There was no disposition on either side to let the fighting interfere with their meals.

[1] I have often seen rebels confined in crates, or cages made of iron of wooden hoops, supported by bamboos, borne on the shoulders of men, and so conveyed to the place of execution, where they have been tossed into the mud, waiting the arrival of the headsman and his assistants to arrange their bodies properly, previous to receiving the fatal, final stroke. I never observed a word uttered or a sigh breathed. They were utterly exhausted, and submitted unmurmuringly to their doom. And I have heard of other cases where men have gone with loud rejoicings to their beheadings.

CHAPTER LIII.

THE DELIGHT OF YAO SIEN ON HEARING THE NEWS.

AND now let us leave the camp and the conquerors, and visit the poor Yao Sien, who was sunk, every day, in deeper and deeper sorrow.

Since the news had reached her of Liang's sad disaster, her tears had never ceased to flow, —they flooded her bosom and drenched her garments.

"From ancient times," she said, "there has been mourning for the dead,—and the mourning is gloomier when we are separated, for the whole of our lives, from those we love; then is man like the cuckoo, whose blood tinges the flowers with scarlet.[1] Woe is me! who look from the balustrade, and see the swallows happily united in pairs, as they fly before me. For me, the world has nothing left to please. He, to whom my faith was pledged, is returned to the yellow waters, and I have nothing to support, nothing to comfort me. Nothing of my former comeliness remains but skin and bones, and the overflowing fountain of my tears will never be exhausted. The flowers fall into the water and are carried away by the stream. Sickness and sadness oppress me, —and whence should comfort come?

"I am wavering and perplexed. My head is wandering, and I dare not leave my bed-chamber, and if, for a moment, my brow is unwrinkled, the phœnix cannot but lament the absence of her mate; and while I sit at the window, I envy the butterflies who sport in couples among the flowers.

"To whom can I unbosom myself but to my chamber maidens? When they are absent, I sit in my loneliness to weep and to wail."

[1] The Chinese believe that, when the end of spring arrives, the cuckoo is so overpowered with his wailings, that blood flows forth from his throat, and, falling on the flowers, gives them a vermilion hue

And in this irrepressible, unbearable torment she passed her days; when, suddenly, Yun Liang entered the room, giggling and laughing, and dancing with joy. "Happiness! happiness! congratulations! Liang is alive. Your honoured father has subdued the rebels. Liang will come to claim my mistress. A messenger is arrived, and has brought the joyful news,—Liang is not dead. Liang has saved himself and overthrown the enemy. Liang will speedily appear in silken garments,—he will appear among us."

Yao Sien answered: "Nay! nay! these must be falsehoods. Do not thus deceive me, and make my bitter woes more bitter. Liang is a wandering spirit in other worlds; he thinks no more of me—or of my troth." Yun Liang only laughed the more: "Did I ever tell a lie from my childhood upward? And when I have heard what is true, shall I not repeat the truth? You will soon see whether I am to be believed."

Yao Sien's spirits revived, and, from that hour, she began again to paint her eyebrows.

CHAPTER LIV.

THE EMPEROR RAISES THEM ALL IN THE RANKS OF NOBILITY.

ENOUGH, for the present, of the ladies, whom we left rejoicing over the glad news. Let us accompany the victory-crowned heroes on their homeward way.

Yao and his uncle were engaged in most animated conversation, and Yao rewarded his curiosity by narrating all the events of the days lately passed. How often Liang had spoken about him, and of all the distress he had felt, on hearing of his being beleaguered in the border city, and how willingly he had offered to sacrifice his life for the General's redemption, and for that purpose had headed the succouring army; how he had himself been surrounded by the rebels in the mountains, and now that a time of peace and rest had returned, it was well he should recognise the sacrifices which had been made on his behalf. The Major-General made a deep and grateful bow, and said: "Seldom is it the privilege of old age to meet with such friendship."

With discourses like these, they reached the Imperial city, and Yang hastened to send in his official report to the Son of heaven.

When the Emperor read it, his dragon countenance brightened: "The energy of this excellent man," he exclaimed, "is indeed most meritorious. Liang swore that he would never submit to the rebels, and Yang has faithfully and loyally defended the frontier-city. Yao has behaved most bravely. Services like these are rare in a thousand ages."

And he issued his Imperial decree, that these three men should be raised to the rank of earldom, and that their descendants should inherit the title, and take up their abode at Court.[1]

After thanking the Emperor for these gracious manifestations, each of them made his arrangements for returning home.[2]

On the arrival of her husband, Lady Yang's sorrow was turned into joy.

But when Yao Sien had saluted her father, she trembled in the presence of her family, and

---

[1] In China, honours are usually conferred on the ancestors, and not on the descendants of those who are raised to nobility. The Imperial decrees fix the titles which are to be given to the progenitors of illustrious men. The reverence of ancestors has been called the natural religion of China, and the ancient sages declare that it is an opprobrium not to know who are our forefathers, for seven generations at least. The ancestral halls, in which the genealogies of the families are kept,—and the division of the people into classes, whose history, for centuries, is a matter of record, as well as tradition, make it easy to trace the origin of all but the humblest classes. As marriages are strictly prohibited where there is any affinity of blood, and the number of family names is few, the lineages are more easily defined; but the honours which belong to the past, are soon absorbed by the influx of newer distinctions, which are the result of the competitive examinations.

[2] Before occupying the posts to which they are promoted, it is usual for the fortunate individuals to return to the place of their nativity,—there to receive, from their families, friends, and neighbours, congratulations on their good fortune. A Chinese proverb says: "The fortunate man brings fortune to all that surround him." Another: "The accumulation of merits, from generation to generation, brings felicity to a whole household."

her forehead did not lose the impress of her anxiety.

The palace was put in order, and all the family gathered together.

Great and wonderful, and beyond example, were the rejoicings with which the news of the Emperor's favour was welcomed.

CHAPTER LV.

LIU REPORTS TO HIS BROTHER-IN-LAW THE EVENTS WHICH HAD OCCURRED.

LIANG, too, after paying his reverential respects to the Emperor, entered upon his homeward way.

But he could not get rid of the misery with which the remembrance of Yao Sien afflicted him. True, he had acquired fame and title,—but what hope had he of being united to his lady-love, for matters in that respect seemed as hopeless as before.

He made acquaintance, however, with a certain Liu, the son of the Minister of the Interior, who came to the provincial city, in order to do honour to the promoted warrior. For he had heard the whole history of his exploits on the frontier, and came to congratulate Liang on his safety and success,—and that, being so young, he had been raised to such rare distinction. But Liu's heart was troubled with sorrow for the loss of his daughter, whose innocent life had been so sadly sacrificed.

Fancying that Liang had no knowledge of the sad event which had happened to young Liu, his daughter went to visit Liang, and narrated to him the whole history.

Liang was touched with sympathy. " What a pitiful story! Why did she not preserve her reputation? Why did she not marry some opulent person? It is very unfortunate for me that I cannot be united to her to the end of my days, for there are very few in the world who are so loveable and so loving as your sister."

When Liu saw that he had carried so much sorrow to Liang, he made a low bow, and took his departure. Liang accompanied him, with the accustomed courtesies, to the door, and returned to his chamber, shedding tears that descended to his outer garment. "How could I have supposed," he exclaimed, "that her love for me was so deep, that she should have drowned herself in the river, because she could not become my wife?"

CHAPTER LVI.

THE EMPEROR TAKES UPON HIMSELF TO BE THE MATCH-MAKER.

HE was so lost in his melancholy reflections, that he did not observe Yang, who had entered his apartment, and asked him the cause of his despondency. "I am the most unfortunate of men," was Liang's reply. "Listen, most honoured Sir! to the tale I have to tell you. Last year, my father promised me in marriage to the daughter of Liu. When I went to the borders, in pursuit of the rebels, she was informed that I had been killed.

"Whereupon, the maiden determined that she would be faithful to her honour and her

13

vow; and when her mother urged her to a second betrothal, she resisted. She flung herself into the water, and was drowned. Her brother has just narrated to me the sad story. Is it a wonder, then, that my heart should be torn to pieces, and that I should turn in despair towards the east wind, which has carried away the Hai Thang branches?"[1]

Hearing this, the General could not restrain his tears: "So much fidelity, in one so young, is seldom to be found, even in the records of ancient times.[2] It was, indeed, a sin and a shame that so pure and beautiful a jewel should have fallen into the abyss. But her name will become illustrious throughout the world. Still, there is no use in your indulging in grief, for what cannot be changed or remedied. My council is, that you should console yourselves,

[1] The *Cidonia Japonica.* A flower, which, like that of the chloranthus, the peach, the lotus, and the almond, is frequently introduced into the love romances of the Chinese. Dr. Hooker informs me that, the plant is generally known in this country as the *Pyrus Japonica.*

[2] The very highest compliment that can be paid, is to declare that, any action equals or exceeds in merit those which illustrate the annals of the past, to which all the Chinese look, not only as the golden age of happiness,—but as furnishing the great models of exalted virtue.

and that you should report the touching history of this incomparable woman to the Emperor himself."

" That is, indeed, an excellent idea, and I will not delay making a report to His Imperial Majesty,[1] and to repair with it to the Court."[2]

He rose early the following morning, and himself presented his memorial at the palace.

This was the answer of the vermilion pencil:

" Chastity like this,—such fidelity and virtue are very rare in this world.   Let a monument

---

[1] The Emperor of China is supposed to be always accessible to his subjects,—to receive, and to read, all the reports that are presented to him.   On those he notices, he writes his decree with the vermilion pencil.   The Emperor's autographs find a ready sale among collectors,—for the autograph collecting passion is as widely spread in China as in Europe.   The Peking Gazettes sometimes contain copies of the memorials which are addressed to the Sovereign, with his remarks thereon.   There are cases in which the memorialists deal very severely with his Majesty, and he condescends to enter upon self-justification.   In our last war, remonstrances were officially printed, which represented that the national disasters were attributable to the neglect and profligacy of the Emperor.

[2] It is a not unfrequent practice, in China, for memorialists to repair to the Court, in order to present their petitions, and to wait for the result.   The paternal relation in which the Emperor is supposed to stand to his subjects, with all whose individual wants and woes he desires to be acquainted, in order to afford redress, is maintained in all the phraseology employed.   On great occasions, he consents to make supplications to the gods, on behalf of the people,—to whom he reports his failures or his successes.

be raised, to send down the history to future generations."

The golden mouth deigned to enquire of Yang: "How many distinguished sons,—how many comely daughters have been born to you?"

Yang held his tablet before his eyes,[1] and reverently replied:

"Your slave has only one daughter, who is

---

[1] Those who are admitted to an audience with the Emperor, carry with them a tablet of about a foot long and three inches broad, which they place before their eyes when His Majesty addresses them. It is not allowed to any one to look on the celestial countenance of the Son of heaven,—no doubt to preserve them from being over-dazzled with its lustre. The tablets are called "Tsao Pan," and have written on them the object of the petition. This is to prevent the necessity of speaking, lest the ears of the "Pure and Holy" should be wounded by any vulgar or unbecoming utterances. I enquired of one of the Viceroys, what passed when he was admitted to the celestial presence. He told me that the Emperor addressed a few words to him in Manchoo, (he being a Tartar) which he answered in the same language. What was said, was a recognition of past services, and the announcement of the new appointment. In all the higher offices, the functionary must repair to the Court, before entering upon his duties. I learnt that the language employed to the Chinese, was the Mandarin idiom, with the Peking pronunciation, which differs considerably from that anciently used when Nanking was the capital. For example: *King*, the metropolitan city, is pronounced *Ching*, in the northern mandarin dialect. *Pe-ching* (which we erroneously write, Pekin) is the capital of the north. *Nan Ching*, pronounced *Nanking*, in the southern idiom, is the capital of the south. The soft *k*, that is, the *k* followed by *e* or *i*, is invariably pronounced as *Ch*, at the Peking Court.

just nineteen years old. She still dwells in the maiden-chamber, and has not yet knit the silken scarlet thread." [1]

The Emperor laughed, and said:

" Well, then, I will undertake the office of Yue Lao,[2] and I give your daughter to Liang for his wife. They must honour one another till they are separated by death; and I hope she will imitate the wife who carried the plate above her eye-brows." [3]

[1] She is yet unmarried.

[2] The Chinese have the proverb : " Marriages are made in heaven," and the divinity, charged with these celestial arrangements, is Yue Lao. Earthly match-makers bear the same name, and the Emperor could very appropriately use it.

[3] The modest wife of Liang Hung was the daughter of Ming, of Yu Fu Fung. Her name was Wang. She was not beautiful, but she was lauded for her eminent virtues, and there were many aspirants for her hand, but she was unwilling to be married.

Her mother reproached her for her prudery, but urged her in vain to consent to be betrothed. She reached the age of thirty, when she answered her mother's entreaties, by saying that she would never marry until she found so deserving a man as Liang Hung.

Liang Hung had never been betrothed, but when he heard of the many excellences of Wang, he asked her in marriage, and obtained the consent of her parents. After the wedding day, she appeared splendidly attired. On being conducted to his house, Liang took no notice of her for seven days. Unable to account for his neglect, she flung herself at his feet, and asked why she was treated with such disregard.

He said, " he had intended La to marry a woman who would be satisfied with plain and simple garments,—to take charge of his household, and not an ornamented, modish doll."

The Emperor sent them magnificent presents of pearls and jewellery, and himself selected an auspicious day for the wedding.[1]

She answered: "I was always accustomed to be simply clad, and if I put on gay apparel, it was because I feared you might be offended if I wore no adornings,—but knowing your pleasure now, I shall willingly doff this gay apparel."

Upon which, she dressed herself in coarse raiment, and changed her name from Kwang (brightness), to Teh Yao, (trembling virtue).

They went together to the Pa Ling mountain, where she provided food for both, by agricultural labour and weaving.

Afterwards, he brought her to Hwui Ki, where he hired himself to attend upon a rice mill. He was only a day labourer, yet she took to him his plate of victuals daily, with hands raised above her eye-brows, that she might not look on his face.

She thus paid to him a most respectful obedience, and, notwithstanding his poverty, treated him with the highest regard.

Wang's history is given in the biographies of virtuous women, as an example of wifely excellence.

A Chinese proverb says: "He, who owes his reputation to his fine garments, is no better than a clothes-horse."

[1] A pretty bridal song is given in the Book of Odes:

Hark! hark! for the voice of the beautiful bird,
Singing hymns from the isle, midst the waters is heard;
He sings to the praise of the modest,—the fair,—
To whom the exalted will look for an heir.
On the top of the stream, as it languishing glides,
The lotus flowers dance up and down with the tides.
On the banks, the sweet maiden is walking,—and he
Is sighing,—not sleeping,—but seeking. 'Tis she—
'Tis she,—whom he seeks,—yet he cannot discover,
But restless he longs, and still looks for his lover.
But the lotus flowers dance on the top of the stream,
They are dancing, delighted, a welcome for him.

Think of the joy of both, and of their gratitude to the grace of His Majesty, when they returned home to tell the tale to the mother and the daughter. The whole house was full of gladness, and brighter with smiles than any, was the face of Yao Sien, rejoicing in her own happiness, and in the favour of the Son of heaven. She was, in truth, rescued from death. Again she opened her jewel casket,—again she hung up and dusted the phœnix-adorned mirror.

Yun Liang and Pi Yue shared in the general delight. They laughed with one another, and said their mistress would no longer be leaning all the day long with her head upon her hand, taking no care whatever of her eyebrows.

He walks by the stream, and she hears from afar,
The music,—sweet music of lute and guitar.
He gathers the lotus flowers,—wreathes them for her,
Fit offering of worship from love's worshipper.
Hark! hark! drums and bells are rejoicing and ringing,
To her home the sweet maiden the minstrels are bringing.

CHAPTER LVII.

IN OBEDIENCE TO THE IMPERIAL COMMANDS, ARRANGEMENTS ARE MADE FOR LIANG'S WEDDING.

LIANG prepared himself for the wedding, and apparelled himself in his gala garments, ornamented with snakes and dragons. He wore a belt of jasper around his waist, to celebrate the auspicious day.[1]

A great crowd of functionaries and officers escorted him.

[1] The state garments of the Mandarins are very costly, ornamented, according to their rank, with embroideries of dragons, peacocks, storks, serpents, and flowers, both before and behind. They wear silken boots, and caps adorned with a ball of ruby, coral plain or flowered,—light and dark blue,—opaque and transparent glass, gold, unornamented or ornamented,—each marking the grade of honour held by the wearer.

Seldom has there been a display of joy equal to that which was exhibited on the occasion. Surrounded with flowers, the waxen lights were blazing. Bands of music paraded the streets, which were crowded with many colored flags.

All the guests—gentlemen as well as ladies, natives as well as strangers,—whispered to one another: "Wonderful! wonderful! His Majesty,—His Majesty is the Yue Lao.[1] Was there ever such a wonder?"

The loving maiden bore a crown on her head, adorned with phœnixes. She wore a beautiful scarlet wedding robe. Bride and bridegroom were old acquaintances, and they were soon wearied with the noise of the watch-drums.

They retired—to talk over the events of the past year, and to compare their present felicity with their past misery. They paid less and less attention to the interrupting noises, though the songs and the music continued to the break of day. They washed and combed, and offered to heaven their grateful thanksgivings. The

[1] The match-maker.

13 *

face of the bridegroom was bright as if he had been one of the genii; that of the bride, lovelier than the countenance of a fairy. Pi Yue and Yun Liang were retained in the lady's service, and the dread of separation no longer afflicted the happy pair.

CHAPTER LVIII.

MR. LUNG PRESENTS A MARRIAGE MEMORIAL TO HIS MAJESTY.

LIVELY and happy, as fishes in water, were the united pair, but we have something to say of the Examiner, who had arrived at the capital city.

He had become the provincial treasurer of Peking, and he had heard the whole of Liang's history. Returned home, he thus addressed his wife and the young Lady Liu.

" Liang has been victorious. He has annihilated the rebels. The report of his death, which every one believed, turned out to be a falsehood. A memorial monument is ordered to be raised,—and only think! it is to be for our adoptèd daughter. The Emperor made himself the match-maker, and has allowed him to marry.

"What can now be done? I will go to Court to-morrow. I will ask for an audience from the Emperor, and lay the whole matter before him." [1]

Yu Khing bowed, and said: " Take no trouble, father! he is now wedded to another maiden, and I will think no more about binding my hair. Let him enjoy his happiness and leave me to my affliction."

The old lady said, laughingly: "Nay! my pretty maiden! You speak without considera- tion. He cannot have forgotten your good- ness,—he proclaimed everywhere your virtues; but as the Emperor has become the match- maker, we are in his hands. But we both counsel you to bind up your hair."

---

[1] Prostrate reverence, before parental authority, is laid down in the Chinese codes as one of the primary social obligations. Mis- conduct or disobedience on the part of a son, is said invariably to bring down curses upon the father or mother. It was quite in the natural course of things that Lung should appeal to the Emperor, and that the Emperor should require that the marriage contract entered into by the father, should be respected by the son.

Not a word of answer did Yu Khing give; but when night came, she bade them farewell, and withdrew to her chamber.

The treasurer went early next day, asked an audience, and delivered his memorial to the Emperor, who burst into laughter, and said: " What wonderful things happen in this world! Liang shall also marry the other girl."

And so he gave his sanction to the union; he gave to each the rank of legitimate wife, and ordered that the second wedding should be celebrated with all the festivities and demonstrations which had accompanied the former, and that the celebration should take place without delay.

CHAPTER LIX.

YAO SIEN RECOMMENDS HER HUSBAND TO MARRY YU KHING.

WHEN the mandate of the Emperor had been communicated to Liang, he left the Court, and returned home, to convey to his beloved the important news. He entered her chamber, calling out: " Yao Sien! I have somewhat to tell you, which may not be pleasing,—but is most wonderful. Yu Khing is not dead. She was rescued from drowning, and is now alive in Peking. His Majesty has been pleased to order that I should marry her."[1] " What! "

---

[1] It need scarcely be here remarked that, the will of the Emperor is a peremptory law, and that, in his decision that Liang should espouse Yu Khing, after he had sanctioned the marriage with Yao Sien, there was nothing which is not wholly accorded with Chinese habits and with the patriarchal polygamic usages which still prevail.

Yao Sien answered, " When the dragon was surrounded by the waters,[1] the young lady, for the love of you, flung herself into the river, willing to sacrifice her life. Her exemplary purity and faithfulness are known to all the gods, and now that you are wedded to me, you speak so coldly of her virtues. But His Majesty has settled the matter. I will be your hand-maid,—it is fitting that we be divorced."

Liang sweetly smiled: " Was there ever such disinterested virtue? Rare, indeed, is it in this world."

[1] A common phrase, to express a difficult or embarrassing position. In this case, referring to the beleaguering of Liang by the rebels.

CHAPTER LX.

THE TWO PHŒNIXES ARE UNITED.

THE arrangements were all made for the celebration of the second marriage in a style as magnificent as for the first. The treasurer, an opulent man, provided a splendid and costly trousseau for his daughter. After the ceremony was over, the two brides embraced one another as sisters, and though Yu Khing was a year older than Yao Sien, they felt kindly one towards the other, nor was there a shadow of jealousy between them. Liang took the chamber-maids, Yun Liang and Pi Yue, as his concubines, and they both bare children to him.

He invited his parents to Peking. Tears of

joy dropped upon his mother's garments, when she looked back on the past, and exclaimed: "I feared that we had been separated from our son for ever, and now we are so happily united. Thanks to the gracious favour of His Majesty, we have now two beautiful daughters-in-law, more beautiful than Si Chi herself, so that our children, and children's children, will occupy an honourable rank, and be happy for generations to come."

Since that day, the house has been full of felicity, and favouring zephyrs will render the house fragrant for a thousand years.

There came, also, a message that the old gentleman, Liu, had arrived. As soon as Yu Khing received the message, she bade farewell to her parents-in-law, in order that she might accompany her mother home.

She wore a crown, adorned with a phœnix; she was clad in a scarlet robe, and followed by twenty serving-maids,—each one excelling the others in comeliness,—and all were clad in silken garments.

Over the head of the bride, a stately canopy of fragrant aloe wood was carried, and ten men slaves followed after. Other servitors carried the Imperial axes, and the ceremonial staves,[1] while banners and tablets of gold, directing the way to be cleared, were lifted high above.

And in this grand style they reached the house of Liu.

The old gentleman was seated in the hall, and seeing the procession approach, he said to himself: "Who can be visiting me with all this pomp and state?" When, raising his head, his eyes fell upon his daughter. He fancied it was a dream, and almost stretched his eyes out of their sockets,—but he could not be mistaken, —this beautiful woman could be nobody but his daughter. He sent instantly for his wife, to come and welcome their child, whom seeing, she cried out with passionate affection:

"Well do I repent me of my former injustice!"

Yu Khing narrated all that had occurred,— and joyful tears absolutely drenched their garments.

"O auspicious day!" exclaimed the old

[1] The ceremonial staves are painted scarlet, and are headed with a golden melon.

lady, "the day of our re-union has dawned. We will forget all the past,—it shall never be mentioned more,—let us rejoice together in the promotion of our daughter, whose virtuous chastity will every where be proclaimed."

The father and son-in-law exchanged congratulations—with wishes for mutual happiness, especially remembering Yao Sien, the lady of the jasper lake.

They conveyed to the examiner, Lung, the expressions of their deepest thankfulness,—and they have all lived together harmoniously, like blood relations. Liang and his wives were supremely happy,—their only rivalry being in beauty and grace.

Sometimes, in the bright moonshine, they go and drink wine together. Sometimes, in the cool breeze, they address complimentary verses to one another.

Indeed, it would be impossible to enumerate all their felicities.[1]

---

[1] Though, in many respects, the social habits of the Chinese resemble those of the oriental world, influences exist, far stronger than prevailed among Hebrews or Mahomedans, which account for the plurality of wives and concubines, so common in China. A certain shame and infamy attaches to the childless, and no anticipa-

tion is more terrrible than the absence of descendants, whose duty
it is to perform those rites which are deemed necessary to the repose
of the manes of the departed, and whose neglect will compel the
perturbed spirit to be a wretched wanderer,—restless and homeless
through the world. Many Chinese ethical authorities insist that a
motherless wife should not only allow a second marriage or alliance,
but that it is her bounden religious duty to recommend, and, in case
of need, to provide a second wife or concubine, in order that her own
spirit may not be perturbed after death, and that, during life, she
may not be haunted by the thought that she had made no provision
against the saddest of calamities. One writer especially recommends
the wife to select a young, beautiful, and attractive maiden, and to
make her home comfortable and captivating.

My experience leads me to doubt whether, on the whole, these
domestic arrangements are a source of felicity.   Sure I am that
social life in China is, on the whole, less happy than among ourselves.
I once travelled with an opulent Hong merchant, who told me he
had sixty wives and mistresses. I asked whether there was not
much jealousy in his household, and whether he distributed his
attentions so as to establish a tolerably general satisfaction among
the ladies. He said: "No! for that he had a special preference for
'No. 7.'" She, in truth, was the prettiest of the whole.

The Roman Catholic Missionaries in China have often told me
that, if their influence had gone no farther than to confine their
converts to a single wife, they thought they had done much for the
civilization and domestic felicity of their followers.

The finale of our Novel does not quite accord with Sir John Davis'
opinion—always highly to be appreciated, that, under no circumstances, can it be allowed to a Chinese to have more than one wife.
Yao Sien undoubtingly consents, after her marriage, to be considered
as the concubine of Liang, but Imperial authority raised her to the
same conjugal rank as Yu Khing, and "the two phœnixes" are in-
stalled in the possession of equal wifely privileges. Handmaids are—
as in the case of the attendants of Yao Sien, selected from the inferior
classes, and may be purchased in the open market,—but both the
brides in our Novel belonged to the higher orders. The title of a
well-known play, is *Tan Lwan Shwang Fung Twan Yuen*, or, "The
perfect happiness of the bridegroom and his two wives," (Chinese

Courtship), and there is another well-known Drama, *Sien Fung Lwan*, "Three brides and a bridegroom."—*Thom's Lasting Resentment*, p. 80.

The position of a concubine in China is not one of opprobrium, but resembles that of the "hand-maid" of patriarchal life, as seen in biblical history.

In the "Perfect Collection of Domestic Gems," the author addresses himself to those childless wives, whose "malignant jealousies" prevent the continuation of the family race. "Not only do you injure your husband by cutting off his generation,—you stop the ancestral sacrifices,—and when his helpless old age is come, you will bitterly repent, for you will discover that you have wronged not only him, but your own selfish self, for who shall take charge of your coffin? Who shall bring libations and offerings to your tomb? The cup of bitterness which you prepared for another, you yourself will be compelled to swallow. I beseech you to act discreetly and virtuously, and provide, cheerfully and honestly, a handmaid for your husband." In most cases, the wife is a consenting party to these household arrangements,—for, though the children are deemed legitimate, the mother remains in a state of vassalage to the No. 1 wife. One of our female servants at Hong Kong, a professing Christian, told us that, during a projected absence, she had made proper provision for her husband's social comfort, and expressed great astonishment that we should see anything improper in the arrangement.

Mencius says : "To be wanting in filial piety is the greatest sin of youth,—to be childless, is the greatest misery of age."

LEWIS & SON, SWAN BUILDINGS, MOORGATE STREET.

www.ingramcontent.com/pod-product-compliance
Lightning Source LLC
Chambersburg PA
CBHW060546030726
47498CB00005B/1294